92 Park Street · Adams, MA 01220
phone · 413 743-8345

★★ "Did I read this already?" ★★
    Place your initials or unique symbol in
square as a reminder to you that you have
read this title.

7-1-13	Dick	Great	author		

JUNCTION FLATS DRIFTER

JUNCTION FLATS DRIFTER

•

Kent Conwell

AVALON BOOKS
NEW YORK

Published by Thomas Bouregy & Co., Inc.
160 Madison Avenue, New York, NY 10016

Library of Congress Cataloging-in-Publication Data

Conwell, Kent.
    Junction Flats drifter / Kent Conwell.
        p. cm.
    ISBN 978-0-8034-9830-3 (hardcover : alk. paper)
    I. Title.

PS3553.O547J86 2007
813'.54—dc22

                              2006038405

PRINTED IN THE UNITED STATES OF AMERICA
ON ACID-FREE PAPER
BY HADDON CRAFTSMEN, BLOOMSBURG, PENNSYLVANIA

To my grandson, Keegan, and to Amy and Jason,
his parents, whose lives will never be the same.
And to my wife, Gayle.

Chapter One

The rising sun dusted the clouds on the horizon with a thin veil of red against a brittle blue sky. Tiny sparrows and mockingbirds sang gaily, welcoming the coming day. Down in the arroyo on the side of the mesa, Josh Barkley pushed the war from his mind for the thousandth time as he squatted by the small fire and poured himself a cup of steaming six-shooter coffee. He slid the battered pot back in the red-hot coals, the heat from which drove the chill of the crisp October morning from his bones.

An urgent grunt jerked his head around.

On the rim of the arroyo, Mike Gray-Eyes crouched behind a mesquite as ancient and wrinkled as the old Indian himself. His black eyes fixed intently on the shallow valley below, he grunted again.

Josh frowned. "What?"

1

The old man nodded to the valley. "Trouble."

Hastily setting his tin cup on the ground, the lanky cowpoke clambered up the steep arroyo slope to the old Indian, flipping the leather loop from the hammer of his Navy Colt as a precaution. He knelt beside Mike Gray-Eyes and peered down into the valley far below where two wranglers pushed a small herd of beeves to the west.

Less than a quarter mile behind the herd, three riders raced through the mesquite, revolvers drawn. Moments later, half-a-dozen distant pops broke the crisp morning, silencing the bright songs of the morning birds.

The herd bolted. The two wranglers turned to fight off the rustlers, but their startled horses reared, unseating one cowpoke and throwing off the second puncher's aim. In the next instant, he threw up his hands and tumbled over the rump of his horse as if a giant hand had knocked him backward. The first cowboy, afoot now, grabbed for his six-gun, but before he could get off a shot, a hundred and eighty grain lead plum slammed him to the ground.

One of the three rustlers reined up, put finishing slugs in the two downed cowpunchers while the other two raced after the herd.

Stunned at the suddenness of the attack, Josh watched helplessly as the three owlhoots disappeared into the mesquite in pursuit of the stampeding cows.

Mike Gray-Eyes grunted and struggled to his feet. Leaning on his crutch, the old Kickapoo glanced down at the small, smokeless fire. "Coffee smell good."

Muttering a curse, Josh slid down the side of the arroyo. "Forget the coffee. Those two need our help."

"Them two dead. Drink coffee while hot."

"I'm going out there to see about them."

Mike stared up at him and shrugged. "Do no good."

Josh snorted and quickly saddled his buckskin, keeping one eye on the pony's head that was turned in his direction and the other on the saddle. "You best watch it, Buck. You bite me again, you broomtail, and you'll wish you hadn't," he growled, jerking the cinch tight. The buckskin didn't attempt to bite, but the deep-chested pony did crow hop a few times in a weak effort to unseat Josh after the lanky cowboy swung into the worn saddle. He clicked his tongue and touched his spurs to the gelding's flanks, sending the powerfully built animal scrambling up the side of the arroyo and racing toward the fallen men.

Mike Gray-Eyes had been right. The two cowpokes were dead.

Their horses had run only a short distance, so within minutes, Josh rounded them up. After leading them back to the two wranglers, he dismounted and tied his buckskin to a mesquite.

He threw the bodies over the saddles and tied ankles to wrists under the horses' bellies. He started back around to his buckskin, but halted abruptly before walking behind Buck. Seconds later, the buckskin let out with a powerful kick, but all he managed to hit was air.

Josh grunted, and with a wry grin muttered. "I ain't

that stupid, horse. Just wait until I got the time, and I'll break your carcass from that biting and kicking.

Back at the camp, Josh tied the two horses a short distance from the fire and squatted to savor a cup of steaming coffee. "Best I can figure," he muttered to Mike Gray-Eyes. "Junction Flats ought to be a couple hours ride to the south. We'll take those two down there."

The expression on the old Kickapoo's ancient face was as unreadable as a card shark when he replied. "Much trouble."

They broke camp with Josh trailing the two horses. Buck decided he didn't much care for the horses tagging so close behind him on the limestone cobbled road, so each time one drew too close, he aimed a kick at it until Josh finally unrolled his lasso and strung out a longer lead rope.

He glanced at Mike Gray-Eyes. "That'll stop this ornery critter," he announced with smug satisfaction.

Mike grunted. "You make bad trade for horse. He *"astuto coyote, malo*, sly animal, mean, no good."

At twenty-eight, Joshua Edward Barkley had grown up with horses, riding since before he could remember. A lanky, wiry young Texan, he had no doubt there was not a single horse pounding the range he could not tame. With a confident grin, he replied. "Don't worry. I'll take care of this one. He's the best pegger I've run across. I've seen one, maybe two cowponies like him that can cut on a biscuit and not break the crust." He paused and added. "He's going to be worth the trouble. Don't fret yourself. I'll straighten him out."

The old Kickapoo grunted. "He not be my worry."

Josh arched an eyebrow.

Two hours later, they pulled up beneath a spreading live oak beside the winding road of limestone cobbles. The sun had burned away the chill. Below, the small village of Junction Flats lay along the curving bank of the Llano River. A quarter mile to the west, a wide creek flowed into the river from the north.

A dozen or so buildings made up the town, some of simple board and batten, a few fancier ones of clapboard, and the remainder of rough logs. Smoke curled lazily into the clear, crisp air from a few of the buildings.

Buck stutter-stepped nervously and pulled at the reins. "Easy, boy, easy. Yonder must be Junction Flats, Mike," Josh said. "Let's get on down and see if anyone can put a name to these hombres."

The old Kickapoo's wrinkled face grew grim. His black eyes surveyed the small town warily, noting the few figures on the streets. After a moment, he announced ominously, "Town is bad."

Josh snorted. "Nonsense. Let's ride in. We'll drop these jaspers off and see if I can pick up some work. I'm just about busted." He patted his pocket. "We don't have enough *dinero* to get us on down to San Antone." He clicked his tongue and urged his pony down the nar-

row road, staying between the ruts cut by the iron
wheels of wagons.

Reluctantly, Mike Gray-Eyes followed, his keen,
black eyes constantly quartering around the town and
uneasy prickles of dread running down his spine.

A few curious eyes narrowed as they rode in, two
strangers garbed in Western dress, jeans, light jackets,
and floppy hats. One was white, the other either
Mexican or Indian, neither of which was welcome in
Junction Flats.

Josh reined up in front of the sheriff's office. Mike
Gray-Eyes stopped a few feet behind his younger partner, well out of reach of Buck's kick. Moments later, a
tall man with narrow shoulders, a drooping mustache
speckled with gray, and a belly the size of a watermel-
on lumbered from the jail. He looked from Josh to
Mike Gray-Eyes, then his eyes grew hard when they
settled on the two bodies draped over the saddles.

Josh spotted the star on the man's chest. "Howdy,
Sheriff."

With a curt nod, Sheriff August John Rabb grunted.
"Howdy." His cold eyes went back to the dead men.

"Name's Josh Barkley. This here is Mike Gray-Eyes.
We picked up these hombres about two hours out." He
briefly explained the circumstances as the sheriff
inspected the two bodies. "This being the closest town
I knew of, I figured I best bring them here. You recognize them?"

Sheriff Rabb looked up suspiciously. "Tom Green and Burt Wilson. They rode for the Circle B." He cut his eyes at Mike Gray-Eyes, his face reflecting his skepticism. "Where did you say the rustling took place?"

"Back north. A couple hours. We camped the night in an arroyo on the side of a mesa. The rustlers hit just after sunrise."

Rabb chewed on his bottom lip. "That'd be Wild Horse Mesa. Only one north of here that close."

"If you say so."

The sheriff studied them a few moments. "Reckon you're telling it straight, otherwise you'd have left them laying out there for the buzzards." He nodded, his voice mellowing. "Much obliged for your trouble, Mr. Barkley." His eyes flicked to the old Kickapoo, then back to Josh. "Whereabouts you from?"

Josh shrugged. "Ever'where, nowhere."

Sheriff Rabb arched an eyebrow. "Where you heading?"

The young cowboy eyed the sheriff narrowly, piqued by his inquisitiveness. "Ever'where, nowhere," he replied impulsively instantly regretting his flippant response.

The sheriff's eyes grew cold.

Josh gave him a disarming smile. "Sorry, Sheriff. I don't mean to rile you. I just ain't used to answering questions, but, I understand. It's your job." He nodded to the old Indian. "Mike and me, we're heading for San Antone. Hear some jasper by the name of Shanghai

Pierce might be putting together a herd next spring to head up to Kansas or Colorado."

Sheriff Rabb snorted. "You're a few months early, ain't you?"

"Maybe so. You heard the old saying about the early bird and the worm. Well, sir, I sure hope it's true. Of course, I got to find us something to tide us through the winter."

Nodding tersely, the sheriff hooked his thumb over his shoulder. "Come on inside and write out your statement for the inquest."

Josh glanced at Mike Gray-Eyes who lifted an eyebrow questioningly, indicating that neither did he have any idea what an inquest was.

"What's that inquest thing you're talking about?" Josh asked the sheriff.

"Sort of a legal hearing. Makes sure the law knows just what happened to them jaspers."

Josh glanced around at Mike. "I'll be right back, then I'll see about finding someway to pick up a few dollars so we can be on our way."

Sheriff Rabb looked around sharply at Josh, but said nothing.

Inside the sheriff's office, Josh wrote out the events of the morning and signed the document. He handed it to the sheriff who simply glanced at the document before slipping it in the top drawer of his battered desk. "Appreciate it, Mr. Barkley." He looked up, his voice growing cool. "Now, a word of warning. I heard you say you planned to look for a job temporary like. Well, I reckon you might be smart to ride on. I don't have no feelings one way or another about your friend out there, but this town hates Injuns. Just two weeks ago, Comanche massacred some of the town's citizens about ten or twelve miles up Viejo Creek."

Josh nodded over his shoulder. "That the creek back west of town?"

"Yep. That's where the town got its name, Junction Flats. The junction of Viejo Creek and the Llano River." He cut his eyes to the door. "Like I say, it ain't healthy for redsticks around here."

Josh narrowed his cold green eyes, studying the sheriff carefully. "Mike Gray-Eyes is Kickapoo, Sheriff. Kickapoo means wanderers. They don't fight unless pushed into it. Never have. That's where the name came from. Besides, the old man's crippled up something fierce. Got to have a crutch to get around."

Sheriff Rabb stroked his gray mustache. "Makes me no mind as long as there ain't no trouble, but I know these folks around here, Mr. Barkley. They don't give no nevermind what kinda Injun one of them redsticks is. They's all Injuns, and that's how folks around here think of it."

Before Josh could reply, a gunshot boomed from outside. Both men rushed from the jail and jerked to a halt on the boardwalk.

Two young cowpokes, not yet in their twenties, held six-guns pointing up at the old Kickapoo Indian sitting astride his pinto, which, undisturbed by the gunfire, appeared to be dozing. "I told you to climb down, Redstick," one growled.

Sheriff Rabb shouted. "Blast it, Ed Carson, Red Harper! You boys holster them six-guns and get out of here before I throw you both in jail. Better yet, I'll tell your old man."

"Back out of this, Sheriff," Red shot back, keeping his eyes on Mike Gray-Eyes. We're going to have us a little payback here."

Stepping off the boardwalk, Josh started toward the two, who stood a few feet behind the old Kickapoo. "Now, hold on, boys. We rode in wanting no trouble. You just back away, and we'll ride on out."

Young Ed Carson snorted. "This ain't none of your business, cowboy. Just you stop right where you are."

Slowly, Josh continued toward them. Young Carson jerked his six-gun around on Josh, and the cocking of the hammer sounded like a cannon.

Chapter Two

The sheriff barked. "Ed!"

Red turned his six-gun on the sheriff. "This ain't your affair, Sheriff."

Across the street, a wizened old man, crippled by arthritis, hobbled out of the livery. He halted by the water trough, watching the drama unfold.

Josh held out his arms and gave a shy grin as he continued, altering his direction obliquely to swing around the two gunnies instead of approaching them directly. "Look, boys. I just want to talk." From the corner of his eye, he spotted Buck cock his head and look back over his shoulder. He sure hoped that hammer-headed buckskin was still in a kicking mood.

From the top of his pinto, Mike Gray-Eyes suppressed a smile.

"I told you to stop, cowboy," Ed Carson barked.

"Look at me," Josh said. "I got my arms out. I just want to talk to you before you do something you'll regret the rest of your life. I know about making big mistakes. Why do you think I'm drifting?"

Sheriff Rabb lifted an eyebrow.

Red kept his gun on Mike as Ed Carson frowned at Josh, who by now had eased around and stopped several feet directly behind his ornery buckskin, placing the two hotheaded cowboys directly between him and Buck. The young cowpoke sneered. "Killing redsticks ain't no regret to me."

"Maybe not, but this old man is crippled up something bad." He paused, took a step toward Carson and continued. "He can't hurt a soul. He's helpless as a papoose. Why, I even got to help him up and down on his pony. Sometimes I even got to gum his meat for him." He kept his eyes on the young cowpoke, knowing that if he glanced up at Mike Gray-Eyes, he'd see fire shooting from the old Kickapoo's black eyes at the lies Josh was spouting.

Sheriff Rabb shouted. "Barkley. Back away."

Taking another step forward, Josh replied in a calm voice. "The boy's just nervous, Sheriff. He don't plan on hurting anyone."

Ed Carson stepped backward. He jabbed his six-gun at Josh. "I told you to stop. I'll blow your head off if you don't."

"No, you won't, Ed. I'm white. You might get by killing an Indian here in Junction Flats, but what about a white man?"

Behind the young cowboy, Buck's black tail flicked back and forth, and if a horse's eyes could reflect gleeful anticipation, then it certainly shone in those of that *malo* buckskin.

Young Ed Carson took another step back. He licked his lips nervously and warned Josh again. "I told you to stop."

"Just take it easy, partner. I ain't going to back you into no corner," Josh muttered, easing forward another short step.

The nervous cowpoke swallowed hard and took another step back, then one to the side just as Buck whinnied, threw his hindquarters off the ground, and lashed out with both feet. Young Carson's step to the side is all that saved him from a broken back.

Buck's left rear hoof slammed into the young man's leg, sending him spinning heels over head into the middle of the street before he had time to scream, even before he had time to figure out just what in the blazes had happened.

When Carson finally screamed out, Red jerked around, but Josh had already stepped in and with one hand ripped the six-gun from young man's hand. With his other hand he slammed a knotted fist into the cowpoke's jaw, sending him sprawling unconscious under Mike Gray-Eyes' pinto, which continued to doze with its head drooping, unperturbed by the excitement.

Young Carson writhed in the middle of the dusty street, holding his shattered leg and bawling like a baby.

Josh tossed Red's six-gun to the sheriff as a handful of citizens quickly gathered around the screaming youth, one of them the crippled livery owner. Josh patted his buckskin's neck. "I almost hate to break you of that kicking now, Buck. You sure helped us out this time."

He looked up at the old Kickapoo who curled his lips and snarled. "Papoose? One day, we see who helpless. You no help me up or down my pinto."

By now, the local pill-roller had inspected Carson's leg and ordered some of the curious on-lookers to carry the young man to his office, which was across the street and a few doors down from the jail.

The livery owner, Pappy Roscoe, remained behind, a few feet apart from Josh and Sheriff Rabb as the men gently lifted the moaning cowboy.

Keeping his eyes on the small group hauling Carson away, the sheriff casually remarked, "What mistake was you talking about, Mr. Barkley?"

"What's that?" Josh frowned at the sheriff who was still watching the small party carrying Ed Carson.

"When you told Ed not to make a mistake like you did. The one that put you to drifting." He turned his cool blue eyes on Josh, all lawman now.

The remark caught Josh off guard. For a moment, he stammered. "Mistake?" Then he remembered. "Oh, that," he replied with a laugh. "Blazes, Sheriff. I was just looking for something that would make that hombre stop and think. That's all. I'm drifting because I like drifting." But beneath the laughter, he hoped Sheriff Rabb would drop the subject.

At that moment, a buckboard turned the corner and headed slowly up the dusty street. The driver wore jeans and a heavy coat and a floppy hat that had seen better days. Just before the buckboard reached the cluster of men carrying Ed Carson, the young man suddenly screamed out in pain, startling the horse.

Squealing, the frightened animal reared, pawed frantically at the sky, then lunged into the traces, jerking the buckboard with him as he raced up the street. The smooth-faced driver was shouting and jerking on the reins, but the frightened horse had seized the bit in his teeth and was in full control.

"Look out," Sheriff Rabb shouted.

In three quick strides, Josh reached the middle of the street as the terrified horse shot past.

Paying no attention to the screaming driver, Josh leaped for the panicking horse. He grabbed the cheek piece of the bridle just above the bit, yanked the horse's head to the left, and at the same time, used the horse's momentum to swing onto the animal's back. Still holding the cheek piece, he grabbed the reins with his other hand, and quickly pulled the startled animal to a halt.

"Easy, fella, easy," he whispered, holding the reins tight and his legs firm about the horse's belly.

Moving slowly, he slid off the trembling horse's back, all the while speaking in a soft, soothing voice and caressing the quivering muscles in animal's neck.

Without taking his eyes off the horse, he spoke over his shoulder. "Ease up on those reins, partner. He's calming down. Don't scare him."

A sharp voice shot back. "Who told you to butt in? I had him under control."

Josh jerked around, glaring at the smooth-cheeked driver. Anger surged through his veins. Impulsively, he started for the driver, planning to jerk the ungrateful pup off the seat and kick his pants up around his neck so tight they'd choke him to death.

Sheriff Rabb stepped in and spoke to the driver with a chuckle. "Take it easy, Mary. Barkley was trying to help, and from the looks of it, you needed it."

Josh gaped at the sheriff, then gaped at the driver of the buckboard. Mary? Did he say Mary? He blinked his eyes several times and stared at the driver.

Eyes blazing, she glared at the sheriff. "I told you I didn't need any help, Sheriff. Not from you and especially not from some saddle tramp," she added, her eyes assessing Josh's battered trail garments with disdain.

Her sharp retort bristled the hair on the back of Josh's neck. He shot back. "I might be a saddle tramp, Miss, but at least you can tell I'm a man. Hard to tell what you are wearing them pants."

Mary Simmons' eyes widened in surprise, but before she could respond, an older gent on a dapple-gray horse reined up beside the buckboard. In a deep voice, he called out, "Whoa. Slow down there, girl. This gent here don't deserve no tongue-lashing. From what I just seen, he sure saved your bacon this time."

Jerking her head around, the young woman shot the older man a hard look. "But, Pa—"

Archer Simmons shook his massive head, his shoulder length gray hair flailing behind him. In a stern voice that left no doubt the old rancher expected to be obeyed, he said, "Don't argue, Missy. You just get on down to the general store and pick up our supplies." He glanced at Josh, his face softening into a crooked grin. "Much obliged, Stranger. I'm in your debt." He hesitated, then added, "Don't pay no attention to Mary here. She's got the same sharp tongue as her Ma, rest her soul."

Josh liked the old rancher instantly. He nodded. "Glad I could help, Mister . . ."

"Simmons. Archer Simmons."

"Josh Barkley, Mr. Simmons. Glad I was around."

"Reckon I am too, Mr. Barkley. I got me a ranch a few miles north of town. Be right pleased if you'd take Sunday dinner with us. In fact, if you got yourself a mind to, you could go to services with us Sunday down at the Methodist Church yonder. Reverend Adams is a good man. 'Course, he ain't no hellfire and brimstone preacher, but he do make a body think about the Hereafter."

Mary Simmons snorted and tossed her head "I doubt if Mr. Barkley even knows what a church is, Pa."

Archer Simmons' face froze. "Mary! You watch your tongue. You ain't too old for me to take over my knee, young woman. Now, git and do what I say, or I might just decide to tan your rear right here in the middle of the street."

A crimson blush rose from her slim neck and covered her slender face. Her dark eyes flickered to Josh and the sheriff, the look in them a mixture of anger and embarrassment, then dropped her gaze to the ground. "Yes, Pa," she replied submissively, but Josh could still detect a hint of defiance in her tone. From under her eyebrows, she shot Josh a look filled with red hot coals, then popped the reins on the horses' rump, sending the buckboard up the dusty street.

Archer Simmons shook his head as his daughter drove away. "Been hard raising a girl without a Ma, Mr. Barkley. She can be mighty impulsive-like. Sometimes I got no idea just how to handle her. But, she is a good girl. Now, what about Sunday dinner?"

Josh removed his Stetson and ran his fingers through his close cropped hair. "I do appreciate the invite, Mr. Simmons." He gave the sheriff a faint grin. "But I reckon I plan on riding out."

The old rancher grunted. A grin wide as the Llano River split his sun-browned face. "Well, sir, you take care. If you should happen to hang around, the invite's always open." He touched a gnarled finger to the brim of his John B Stetson and sent his dapple gray after the buckboard.

After Simmons disappeared around the corner, Sheriff Rabb pulled out a twist of tobacco and tore off a length with his teeth and offered it to Josh.

"Thanks, Sheriff, but that's one habit I never picked up."

"Nasty one," Rabb replied. He stroked his mustache

thoughtfully. "I done quit chewing a hundred times, but the flesh was weak." He grunted. "None of my business, but how you fixed for cash, Barkley?"

"Just about busted. Even a Confederate dollar would look good to me now." Josh patted his pocket, and a cloud of dust billowed out.

Rabb laughed. "They ain't worth the paper they're printed on noway. Now, I know what I said earlier, but I been thinking. If you want to hang around a few days and pick up some cash, that's fine with me, but you and your Kickapoo Injun best camp outside of town." He raised an eyebrow. "And he best stay out of town."

Josh glanced up at Mike Gray-Eyes, seeing an imperceptible flicker in the old Indian's eyes that signaled his approval. "Well now, Sheriff. That's right hospitable. I reckon I'll take you up on the offer. Now, all I got to do is find a job."

"Don't suppose that'll be hard, Mister," a voice trembling with age said from behind.

Both men looked around as the crippled livery owner hobbled forward. "I saw what you did out here. I liked what I saw. I can use some help over to the livery. Dollar a day."

Sheriff Rabb frowned. "What's that you say, Pappy? Where's Jimmy Conner?"

The wizened old man squinted up at the sheriff through rheumy eyes. The youngster took a job swamping out McCool's saloon a couple days ago." He looked back to Josh. "What about it?"

Josh grinned broadly and stuck out his hand. "You got a deal, Mister . . ."

"Just call me Pappy. Ever'one else does."

"When do I start, Pappy?"

"First thing in the morning. Four o'clock."

"I'll be there." He turned back to the sheriff. "You got any suggestions where we can camp?"

"Back east along the river." The sheriff gestured with his hand. "About a mile out there's a jumble of rock. You'll find as secure a camp there as anywhere around. I don't figure you'll have any trouble, but I'd keep my eyes open anyway."

As Josh and Mike Gray-Eyes rode out of town, two figures at the saloon window pulled furtively back into the shadows of McCool's Emporium.

Sonora Fats shoved his sombrero to the back of his head and grimaced, his thick, fat lips a bulbous protuberance in his corpulent face. He shrugged his massive shoulders and shot the lean man at his side a hard look filled with cruelty. "I ought to kill those three jaspers you hired. I told them to hide the bodies."

Grat Plummer, skinny as a split rail and with a conscience just as thin, scratched his week-old beard. "You shoulda let me go with them, Fats."

They bellied up to the bar and ordered a shot of Old Orchard Whiskey. After the bartender moved away, Sonora Fats grunted. His massive hand engulfed the glass of whiskey. "Don't worry. I'll make sure they remember next time."

A clever grin spread over Grat's thin face. "What

about them two that brought the bodies in? Think they can identify the boys?"

Fats downed his drink in one gulp and poured another before replying. "They're riding on out. We ain't got no worry."

"What if they come back?"

"Then we still ain't go no worry. They'll be the ones what got the worry."

Grat snickered and downed his whiskey.

Fats grunted and gulped another drink. In the mirror behind the bar, he spotted Reverend Matthew Adams pause at the batwing doors, peer inside, then move on.

"I'll be back directly," Sonora Fats announced, pouring another drink and quickly knocking it down.

Grat's bone-thin face frowned. "Where you going?"

"None of your business. The others get here, tell them to wait for me."

Half-a-mile east of Junction Flats, Josh turned north. Mike Gray-Eyes followed without comment. After a few yards, Josh spoke over his shoulder. "You ain't got nothing to say about me turning off the trail the sheriff sent us on?"

Mike grunted. "Me do same."

Josh laughed. "Reckon you would have too." He paused, then added. "Reckon the sheriff's a good man, but I'd just as soon no one know where we make our camp."

The old Indian grunted. "You make good Kickapoo."

The leather-tough cowpoke looked around, a hint of surprise in his eyes.

Before he could reply, Mike Gray-Eyes added, "Maybe."

Chapter Three

From where he stood gazing out the jailhouse window with a cup of coffee in hand, Sheriff Rabb watched curiously as Sonora Fats lumbered down the boardwalk on the far side of the street. He suspected Fats and his rowdy sidekicks of the rustling going on in the surrounding counties, although he had yet to discover one shred of evidence to support his suspicions. But he was looking. And if they made the mistake of hitting a herd in his county, he'd grab them faster than a weasel can rip off a chicken's head.

"Until then," he had explained to Reverend Adams when the preacher had questioned such disreputable owlhoots' presence in Junction Flats. "I got to treat them like anyone else. They done nothing wrong here, I can't do nothing to them."

Sonora Fats stepped off the boardwalk and crossed

the street toward the Methodist Church. Rabb's frown deepened. "Now what the Sam Hill is a no-good like that hombre going to the church for?"

He watched as Fats closed the church door behind him, making a mental note to ask the reverend what Fats' business had been.

From where he stood in front of the pulpit, Reverend Matthew Adams' eyes narrowed when Sonora Fats closed the door. Fats hesitated, and when he spotted the slender preacher, his thick lips twisted in an amused sneer. Their eyes locked, and neither man spoke for several seconds.

Finally, the preacher hissed. "Why did you have to come through the front door? Everyone in town could see you."

Sonora Fats rubbed his burgeoning belly. His tone heavy with sarcasm, he replied, "Maybe I got tired of coming through the back door." His sneer broadened. He continued before the reverend could respond. "Keep your shirt on. Just tell them I wanted my soul saved or something. You're the preacher. You got the words."

Instinctively, Reverend Adams' right hand drifted down to his hip, only to remember that he no longer wore a six-gun.

Sonora Fats laughed. "What's the matter, little brother? You wishing for the old times?"

"Don't call me that. You're no brother of mine. I told

you I'd keep quiet about you, but that was before the murder of those two men back north of town."

Pushing his battered sombrero to the back of his head, Fats laughed and sauntered lazily down the aisle. His eyes glittered with amusement. "So what are you going to do, run over there and tell the sheriff that your big, bad brother killed them two jaspers? You do, and you'll stir up more trouble than you can handle."

Reverend Adams glared at his brother defiantly.

Fats laughed. "On top of that, you got any idea what'll happen to you if this town finds out you're a Confederate deserter?"

Matthew Adams doubled his fist. He wanted to slam the sneer on his brother's fat lips down his throat.

The leer on Sonora Fats' lips faded. "Look, Matt. For your information, that was none of my doing. I told you that I had a small place back west of here. I'm staying honest. I don't want no truck with Sheriff Rabb. Whatever is going on around here ain't none of my doing— not the rustling, not them killings." He paused, staring levelly at the preacher, daring him to dispute the explanation.

Skepticism filled Adams' eyes. "Hard to believe that it's only a coincidence. Just last week, I told you about Bartholomew's herd. Now the herd was rustled and his men got killed."

Fats grunted. "Yeah, you told me, but like I said, that wasn't me or my boys. I'm keeping things straight here in Junction Flats. Why, I'm even working for McCool from time to time."

Adams' eyes narrowed. "You telling me the truth, Elm?"

Fats grinned. "I ain't lying. I don't want no trouble here in town, Matt. Me and the boys is trying to make a go of it. Like I told you when we first met up here last summer, I ain't stupid enough to do nothing wrong in Sheriff Rabb's town and cause me trouble. I just want to build a small place and find some peace."

Adams cut his eye toward the saloon. "Why McCool? Why you working for him?"

Fats scratched at the three-day-old beard on his heavy jowls. A crooked grin twisted his lips. "He's the only one who'll hire us." He paused, and his voice grew bitter. "Town folks hereabouts don't cotton much to those who might have made mistakes in their early days." He paused, then added, "I reckon you can testify to that, can't you?"

For a moment, Matt Adams studied his brother. He cleared his throat. "I'm not proud of my past either, Elmer. But I've straightened things out with the Lord." He hesitated when he saw the flare of skepticism in his brother's eyes. "Don't laugh. You might not believe in God, but I do. I got my life going in the right direction. I pray for you, Elm. I pray you'll leave town. I don't want anything bad to happen to you ever, but I want you out of town so both of us can get on with our lives."

Fats listened in amusement. "You was always the weak one, Matt. You ain't changed. But don't worry. If I have a good year, I plan on selling out. It'll be *adios* Texas, hello San Francisco. Until then, I ain't causing no one no trouble."

"I hope so, Elm. I truly hope so."

Sonora Fats had a cruel streak as a youth, and as he grew, the streak grew with him. When he departed the church moments later, he deliberately left the church door open so his brother could watch as he stopped on the porch, faced the church, knelt, and still wearing the amused sneer on his round, greasy face, facetiously made the sign of the cross.

Inside, Reverend Matthew Adams kicked the door shut.

Moments later, a knock sounded at the back door.

When the preacher opened the back door, Lester Boles, the postmaster, pushed past him.

A slight, short man, Boles looked up at the reverend. Alarm etched lines of concern in the small man's face. "What was that outlaw doing in here?"

Momentarily confused by the unexpected question, Adams hesitated, then feigned innocence. "Who? The one they call Sonora Fats?"

Boles nodded emphatically. "Everyone in town saw him come in here."

Then Adams recognized the drift of the small man's concern. Glibly, he lied. "He's Catholic. He was wondering if I, being a Protestant minister, could give him absolution, that's all."

For a moment, Boles studied him. "That's it? That's all?"

"Certainly. What did you think?"

Boles shook his head and plopped down like a sack of potatoes on the front pew. "I didn't know what to think." His voice dropped lower. "You know, we can't take any chances."

With a trace of contempt in his eyes, the reverend stared down at the smaller man. "You don't have to tell me about taking chances, Lester. I know exactly what this town would do to us if they found out we were Copperhead spies."

Boles grimaced up at him. "Don't say Copperheads. I don't like the word."

A crooked grin ticked up one side of Adams' lips. "But that's exactly what we are, Lester. You and me, we're blue-blooded, well-paid Yankee spies, Copperheads." He took the smaller man under the arm and gently helped him to his feet. "Now, it's best you get back to the post office. After all, we don't want anyone to wonder why the postmaster is over at the church during working hours, do we? Might make them suspicious. And then you know what would happen to us," he added with a trace of black humor.

Sheriff Rabb paused in the middle of the street when he spotted Lester Boles leaving the church. He frowned. He'd been standing at the window from the time Sonora Fats stepped inside the Methodist Church and until he departed. He hadn't seen the postmaster enter the church, so he must have gone in through the back door. Curious, the old lawman told himself. Why would Lester use the back door? Mighty curious.

Josh's eyes popped open. He stared at the starry heavens above, straining his ears for whatever had awakened him. Then he heard it, the thunder of hooves rolling across the rocky hills and through the spreading live oaks, heading east. He turned his head and found the Big Dipper. Midnight.

From the darkness beyond the dead coals of the fire came Mike Gray-Eyes' guttural voice. "Men from town."

"Yeah."

They lay silently, listening and waiting, confident of their own security.

Thirty minutes later, the pounding of hooves returned, slowly disappearing in the direction of town.

When the thunder of hooves had faded beneath the lonely calls of owls and coyotes, Josh rolled over and pulled his blankets about his neck. "They're gone now. Reckon they were a mite disappointed, wouldn't you say?"

Mike grunted. "Me say."

Moments later, the old Kickapoo was sleeping.

Fingers laced behind his head, Josh stared at the stars above. It had been a night like this when he had awakened after the bloody battle with Sherman's troops during Bragg and his Confederate troops running retreat to Ringgold, Georgia.

All about in the darkness was silence, the silence of the battlefield, the silence of the dead. Far to the east came the thunder of artillery.

From April of sixty-one to November of sixty-three, he had fought the Yankees. Six re-enlistments over two and a half years, and how had his loyalty been repaid? His army, his commander, his friends, all had left him for dead.

So, Joshua Simon Barkley, figuring he had done his share of fighting, bound up his wounds and found a stray remount and headed back to Texas.

And since that night, he had fought a daily battle with a guilty conscience.

When Josh rolled out of his soogan just after three o'clock next morning, Mike Gray-Eyes was squatting beside a small fire that lit the boulders surrounding their camp. While coffee boiled, Josh threw a saddle on Buck. The buckskin jerked his head around to nip at Josh, but instead, stuck his tender muzzle into the sharp stick Josh held, anticipating the nip.

Buck snorted at the sudden pain and jerked back.

Josh grinned. "Sooner or later, you're going to learn, boy. Every time you try to nip me, you'll just hurt yourself."

Back at the fire, the old Kickapoo chief nodded to the buckskin. "The *malo coyote*, he bite this morning?"

"Tried." Josh sipped the hot coffee. "Told you that sharp stick would work."

Mike Gray-Eyes grunted.

Josh saw the skepticism in the old man's eyes. He explained. "The pony isn't dumb. As soon as he learns that he'll get hurt every time he tries to nip me or anyone else, he'll stop."

Mike said nothing, just slurped at his coffee, but once, when the old Indian glanced up, Josh saw the doubt in his eyes.

During the night, clouds had rolled in covering the stars. It was dark as midnight under an upside-down skillet, but the buckskin carried Josh along the road without a stumble. Josh grinned broadly into the darkness. The ornery *malo coyote* was as dandy a night horse as he was a cow horse, worth much more than the effort to correct a couple minor flaws like kicking and biting.

The pale light flickering from the barn lantern greeted Josh when he rode into the livery just before four. Giving Josh a gap-toothed grin, Pappy waved him over to where he was sitting beside a pot-bellied stove in the middle of the stall he used for an office. "Put up your pony. Coffee's hot. Drink your fill."

As Josh poured a cup of steaming six-shooter coffee, Pappy drawled. "Hear Red Harper came looking for you last night."

Cupping the tin mug in the palms of his hands, Josh blew gently on the black liquid. "Is that who it was? Heard them, but never saw them."

Pappy cackled. "Just watch out for the boy. He ain't a bad one, but he does got hisself a temper."

Lifting an eyebrow, Josh grunted. "I've seen more than one jasper neck deep in cow chips because of a hot temper."

The next few days, Josh stayed busy. Every night, he and Mike moved camp, each one a little more secure than the previous thanks to the old Kickapoo's scouting the countryside around Junction Flats.

On Saturday, the Simmons' clan rode in to town. Josh watched from the open doors of the livery as Mary Simmons pulled the buckboard up in front of Junction Flats' General Store. Her Pa and one of the brothers reined up beside her.

Pappy paused beside Josh. "That's the little filly you had a run in with the other day, huh?" He cackled.

"Reckon so." Josh grinned down at the old man. "Sure is hot-headed."

"You shoulda knowed her ma. Fact is, I courted Martha, that was Mary's ma, back before Archer won her." Pappy grew reflective, and his rheumy eyes seemed to cloud over even more. "Mighty high spirited, knew what she wanted. Yes, sir, she was one lady that no man would tell what to do if she didn't want to do it."

Josh chuckled and turned back to haying the stalls. "Sounds like that daughter of hers sure didn't fall too far from the tree."

*   *   *

Later, just as Josh finished tossing the soiled hay into the muddy corral and began spreading fresh hay in the stalls, a soft voice cut into his concentration.

"Mr. Barkley."

His pitchfork ready to pick up another bundle of hay, he paused and glanced over his shoulder. A slight figure stood silhouetted in the open doorway. He squinted. "You talking to me, partner?"

The figure stepped forward into a shaft of sunlight from one of the open loft doors above.

Mary Simmons!

Instantly, Josh grew defensive. "Miss Simmons?" The disbelief in his voice was obvious.

She laughed nervously. "I don't blame you for being surprised, Mr. Barkley, but I came to apologize. I was very rude the other day. I spoke out of turn."

Josh hesitated, wondering if old Archer Simmons had indeed taken his daughter over his knee and reminded her of her manners. He studied her a moment. She was wearing buckskins, but despite the streaks of dirt on her clothes and the floppy hat perched on the back of her head, she made a very fetching picture with her long blond hair framing her slender face.

Quickly, Josh yanked his John B from his head. "I should never have said what I did, Miss Mary. I'm the one to apologize."

"Oh, no," she hastily replied, stepping forward. "I was rude. Truth is," she continued, glancing sheepishly at the ground, "I was embarrassed. The horse, Star, did get away with me. I couldn't rein him in, but I was too embarrassed to admit it."

A wave of benevolent feelings flooded over Josh. He leaned on the pitchfork. "That's mighty generous of you to say that, Miss Mary. Tell you what. I'll accept your apology if you'll accept mine."

A bright smile burst across her sun-browned face. She stepped forward and held out her hand. "I'm willing, but only if you'll agree to Sunday dinner with us."

He took her slender hand, feeling the coolness of it under his own rough skin. "Done."

"And church?" She arched an eyebrow in amusement.

Continuing to hold her hand, Josh grunted. "I don't know about that."

She laughed, a bright tinkling that seemed to brighten the day. "All right. I won't hold you to church. We eat around one o'clock. Can't miss the ranch, the Split S. It's out on the north road a few miles."

Chapter Four

When Josh reached the livery Sunday morning at four a.m., he saw that the day would be bright and clear. The cool spell had moved on south, promising a warm day.

Stabling his buckskin, he set about the mundane chores of a livery, feeding the animals, cleaning the stalls, and in his spare time, soaping and oiling tack, cleaning bits, brushing saddle pads.

The morning passed quickly, and at noon, Pappy showed up to relieve Josh for dinner with the Simmons. The old livery owner hobbled to the open doors and pointed to the north road. "About an hour's ride that-away. The road cuts through the middle of Split S. Can't miss the place.

"Obliged. I'll be back in time to close up," he announced, donning a fresh shirt and brushing the dust from his vest and trousers. A final touch was slicking his hair down with water from the wooden horse trough.

He swung into the saddle. The buckskin jittered nervously, anxious to be on the road, and as Josh headed out, he couldn't help wondering which Mary Simmons he would meet today, the rude, sharp-tongued shrew driving the buckboard, or the affable young woman in the livery.

A few miles out, he came upon a rough sawn sign informing riders they were entering Split S land. During the next half hour or so, he passed small bunches of grazing beeves, all wearing the Split S brand. The stock appeared well fed, well cared for.

The narrow road curved through a grove of post oak. As he approached the grove, a rider burst from the shadows and halted in the middle of the road.

Red Harper!

Josh reined up, turning Buck to the right far enough so he could flip the leather loop off the hammer of his Colt unseen.

With a click of his tongue, Red urged his pony forward. He reined up only a few feet distant. "I been looking for you, cowboy." He dragged the tip of his tongue over his lips.

"I've been around."

The young man swallowed hard. "I aim to pay you back for what you did to Ed."

Josh studied him a moment, seeing the fear in Red's eyes. But the determined set to his jaw indicated the youth gunman was bound to follow through with what he figured was an obligation he owed his partner. "I hate to hear that Red. I didn't want any trouble. But, your partner pushed it. He brought it on himself."

Red glared at Josh, his darting eyes reflecting the confusing thoughts tumbling about in his head.

"You want to draw, draw, but I've got to warn you, I'm fast. Too fast for you."

His face paled, but the muscles under the taut skin of his jaw worked like a nest of snakes. He took a deep breath, telegraphing his next move.

He slapped leather, but even before his fingers gripped the butt of his six-shooter, the barrel of Josh's Navy Colt was centered on his chest. He blinked in disbelief, and Josh quickly holstered the six-gun.

With a grin, Red yanked his out, but again, even before he cleared leather, the muzzle of the Navy Colt was pointed at his heart. Josh's words were cold and ominous. "Listen to me, Red, and listen hard. Twice, I could have killed you, and twice, I'm backing away. I won't do it a third time."

For several seconds, Red stared at Josh, his Adam's Apple bobbing up and down in his throat. Slowly, he nodded. "I—I understand."

The cold edge on Josh's words melted away. He holstered his Colt. "Good." With a click of his tongue, Josh rode around the shaken young man and continued his journey.

A few minutes later, Josh caught his first glimpse of the Split S Ranch. He nodded his head in appreciation at the layout. The main house and the outlying buildings were constructed of white limestone, each with a wood shake porch providing shade against the searing Texas sun during the hot seasons, which in that part of the state lasted about eight months. The other four were bitter cold.

Like most of Texas, there were no in-between seasons, just hot or cold.

Half-a-dozen ponies stood idly in the pole corrals while a handful of punchers lolled about in the shade of the spreading live oaks. They all turned their eyes on Josh as he rode in.

Three cowpokes sat on the porch of the main house, watching curiously as Josh rode in. One, a strapping young man, rose and disappeared inside.

The two remaining cowpokes on the porch rose and sauntered to the porch railing as Josh grew near, each taller and heavier built than the first. Moments later, Mary Simmons, wearing a blue gingham dress, her Pa, and the first young man appeared. Archer Simmons raised his hand and called out, "Howdy there, Barkley. Glad you decided to stay around." He glanced at his daughter.

Josh thought nothing of the look the old rancher gave his daughter. "Appreciate the invite, Mr. Simmons." He nodded to the three young men who were studying him suspiciously. "Miss Mary," he added, touching his fingers to the brim of his John B.

Archer Simmons nodded to his sons and drawled. "This here is Kelton, Hammond, and Edward, Kelt,

Hamm, and Ed for short, Mary's brothers. Light and come on in. Cookie's got the grub pile on."

"Howdy." Josh nodded and climbed down.

Mary Simmons hurried to Josh. Tossing her long blond hair, she smiled brightly up at him. "I'm so glad you could make it, Mr. Barkley." She took his arm. "Come with me. I'll show you the way." And without hesitation, she ushered him inside. Leaving her Pa and brothers behind.

Surprised by her friendly and warm manner, Josh allowed himself to be escorted into the stone house as Archer Simmons followed, chuckling.

Mary Simmons swept him through the parlor and into the dining area, a large room with a massive pine table surrounded by a dozen straight back chairs. Mounds of grub filled the table. There were platters of steaks, heaping bowls of succotash, loaves of bread freshly baked, urns overflowing with beans steaming hot, steaming red eye gravy and bubbling mock apple cobbler.

On the table in front of Archer Simmons sat a stack of heavy plates. He surveyed those around the table, bowed his head, muttered grace, and then nodded for his children and his guest to sit.

He then passed out the plates. His sons, Kelt, Hamm and Ed, looked on patiently, but hungrily while Mary served Josh and herself, and then they dug in.

While conversation at meals was usually spare during working days, on Sundays, a more tranquil atmosphere prevailed. The conversation around the table was relaxed and affable. Mary Simmons doted on Josh, much to his discomfort, for he wasn't accustomed to a woman paying him so much attention.

From time to time, he caught the amused glances the three brothers threw each other, covert glances that made him wonder if there was a secret joke among them. Still, he enjoyed the meal and the friendly conversation.

Just as Mary spooned him a bowlful of mock apple cobbler and daubed a heaping mound of fresh cream on it, the pounding of hoofbeats came through the open window.

Archer peered outside and grunted. "It's Hank Bartholomew." He pushed back from the table. "Wonder why he's out on a Sunday?" He glanced at Josh. "You all go on with your meal. I'll be right back."

"What do you figure is going on?" Kelt Simmons muttered, gulping down a chunk of cobbler big enough to choke a horse.

Around a mouthful of grub, his younger brother Hamm replied. "You know old Hank. Any kind of little problem he's got, he comes to Pa."

The youngest brother, Ed, laughed. "Yeah."

Moments later, Archer returned. Outside, the hoofbeats faded away. He slid in at the table and said to no one in particular, "Hank lost some beeves to rustlers. Followed the trail to the buffalo trace, but lost it. Tracked sign about ten, twelve miles, but as usual, it just vanished. He was wondering if we'd lost any beeves."

Josh looked around. "Bartholomew? His brand the Circle B by any chance?"

Archer looked up from his plate. He shifted his mouthful of apple pie to his cheek. "Yep. How come you ask?"

"Curious, I reckon. It was his boys me and my partner hauled in last week."

The brothers exchanged surprised looks. Hamm turned to Josh. "That was you what found old Tom and Burt?"

"Reckon so."

The older brother laid down his knife and fork. His voice took on a cool edge. "Word in town was that the jasper that brought them in was riding with an Injun. That you?"

Ignoring the sudden animosity he sensed in Kelt's tone, Josh grinned at the older brother. "Well, sir, that depends."

"On what?" Hamm demanded.

Archer looked on, a puzzled frown on his face.

Unperturbed, Josh took another bite of cobbler. He chewed slowly, all the while smiling at them. He swallowed the cobbler and touched the napkin to his lips. "Mighty good cobbler, Miss Mary. Mighty good. Now, back to the question you asked, Kelt."

Mary interrupted. "Kelt, you be quiet. Who Mr. Barkley's friends are is none of our business."

Josh stayed her. "Oh, no, Miss Mary. I believe in being open and fair with everyone. Kelt wants to know if that Injun is my partner. Well, Kelt if you can call an old man who's crippled so bad I have to help him on his horse and chew his meat for him an Injun, then yep, reckon he is. Most Injuns I know don't need help from anyone to climb on their ponies or chew their own meat. They'd try to take your scalp if you tried."

"But he's an Injun," exclaimed Ed, staring at Josh in confusion.

"Well, I'm a white man. I didn't pick it, though I reckon I'm glad I turned out that way. Way I see it, Mike Gray-Eyes is just an old man way past his prime. All he wants is a warm bed and a place out of the weather, and when the time comes, a place to die. Truth is, he would have been dead and gone last year when his tribe threw him out to die. But, I found him, and I made him well, and now he tags after me like a grateful puppy." Josh paused. "You going to shoot a broken-down hound dog just because he's old? Nope. Decent folks don't. They'll find a place for him to curl up and stay warm so he can die with some dignity. Isn't that right?"

The three brothers glanced at each other sheepishly, and for several seconds, no one spoke, then Kelt cleared his throat brusquely. "Tell you what, brothers, after a fine meal like this, I feel like some leg wresting to kinda settle all the grub. How about you all?"

His brothers joined him eagerly, anxious to forget the mortification with which Josh's words had filled them.

Josh glanced at Archer Simmons who grinned knowingly and nodded briefly. The old rancher wiped his lips with the linen napkin and pushed back from the table. "What do you say we go out and watch the boys Josh?"

With a knowing grin, Josh rose and held Mary's chair for her. "I think I'd like that just fine, Archer."

Mary excused herself as Josh and her Pa headed outside.

Unlike many of the competitive activities among cowpokes on ranches, leg wrestling seldom escalated into fights or shootings. The worst that could happen was usually a bruised heel, a strained muscle, or maybe a torn shirt as the loser was flipped backward over his head.

As Josh and Archer stepped out on the porch, Kelt and Hamm were situating themselves, lying on their backs, side by side, feet facing in opposite directions.

The game was simple. At the count of one, each man would raise and lower his inside leg, and once again on the count of two. On the count of three, the contestants would lock legs and try to flip his opponent back over his head.

Clearing his throat, Archer warned them. "Okay, boys. No cheating. Remember, no grabbing anything with your hands. Keep 'em flat on the porch. I'll count. Ready?"

Kelt laughed. "Ready."

Hamm chuckled. "Boy, Kelt, I'm going to flip you head over heels today. I got a feeling."

"You always got a feeling, son. You just can't never follow it."

"Wait and see."

Archer called out in a slowly measured beat. "One, two, three!

The two young men locked their legs, each straining mightily to flip the other over. Finally, Hamm gained the advantage, and flipped his older brother backwards.

"Two out of three," shouted Kelt, laughing as he slid back into place.

For the next few minutes, the brothers battled each other, Kelt and Hamm were about even but far superior to their younger brother, Ed, who was as game as a banty rooster, demanding another chance time after time and losing time after time to his older brothers.

After Hamm had taken two out of three from Kelt again, he grinned at Josh. "How about it, Josh? You want to take a chance?"

"Not me." Josh grinned and held up his hand. "You boys are too good for me."

"Not for me," a voice said from behind.

Josh looked around and his jaw hit the floor.

Mary Simmons, decked out in her buckskins, stood in the open door smiling demurely at them. "Okay, who's first," she said, dropping to the porch deck.

Unperturbed by his sister's actions, Kelt nodded to Ed. "Go ahead, little brother. Maybe at least you can beat your sister," he said with a laugh.

"Why not?" Ed dropped to the floor beside Mary.

Josh looked on as Mary and Ed battled. The two siblings were fairly even, but the idea of a young woman engaging in such rollicking behavior with her brothers was a surprise to Josh.

And he was even more surprised when Archer Simmons leaned over and whispered. "Reckon she's a tomboy sure enough, Josh, but mark my words, she'll make some young feller a fine little wife." Josh looked around at the old rancher who winked and added, "Don't you think so?"

All Josh could do was gulp, and nod.

Chapter Five

Mary Simmons unnerved Josh. He didn't mind admitting that fact as he rode away from the Split S later that afternoon. She had been every inch a gracious host and a charming companion, catering to his comfort and ease. And then, she completely shattered the domestic picture by battling her younger brother in leg wrestling—and winning as often as she lost.

He leaned forward and patted Buck on the neck. "You know, Buck, she's a mighty unusual woman, that Miss Mary." The buckskin tossed his head and shook his black mane as if to agree.

Pappy cackled as Josh related the day's events. He slapped his leg with glee when Josh recounted Archer Simmons' remark about his daughter making 'some young feller a fine little wife.' Wagging a crooked finger at the young cowpoke, he chuckled. "You best watch your step. Sounds to me like old Archer's looking to find a husband for that little gal of his."

Josh rolled his eyes. "Well, if he's looking at me, he's looking in the wrong place. Like I've said all along, I'm just passing through. Heading for San Antone."

The next day just before dinner, Mary Simmons, wearing a blue gingham dress, rode in with a large plate covered with a red and white checked cloth. "I didn't reckon that Sunday dinner was apology enough for the other day," she explained with a demure smile, as she handed him the plate.

Stammering out his thanks, Josh reluctantly took the dinner from her hands, at the same time spotting the wide grin on Pappy's face that screamed 'I told you so.'

And regular as a mama cat tending her kittens, Mary Simmons showed up the next three days with covered dinners despite Josh's plaintive plea "I appreciate it, Miss Mary, but you don't have to go to all this trouble."

"I know," she replied. "But I like doing it."

That night around the campfire, Josh announced to Mike Gray-Eyes that he reckoned maybe they should be moving on in the next few days.

The old Kickapoo eyed his young friend shrewdly and shrugged.

Next morning at the livery, Josh saddled Slick McCool's, sorrel. He was leading her out of the stall when Hank Bartholomew rode in.

Pappy greeted the old rancher and introduced him to Josh. Bartholomew forced a grin. "I never got to thank you for hauling in my boys the other day. Mighty decent thing to do."

With a sorrowful frown knitting his brow, Josh looked up at the old rancher. "Wish I could've done something to help your boys or at least to make out the rustlers, Mr. Bartholomew."

"Call me Hank, Son."

"All right, Hank."

A wry grin played over the old rancher's face. "That's been the way my luck's been running lately, I reckon."

Pappy clicked his tongue. "You look like you're hauling around a two thousand pound bull on your shoulders, Hank."

Hank swung down from his gray, his weathered face wrinkled into a frown as rugged looking as the Grand Canyon. "Reckon you about hit the nail on the head," he drawled. "Them rustlers have just about done me in."

Pappy planted his pitchfork in the ground and leaned forward on it. In surprised disbelief, the old livery owner said, "You saying you might be selling out, Hank?"

"Could be. I ain't in Sheriff Rabb's Kimble County, but I come to see the sheriff anyway. Then I find out he's over to Squaw Creek for a couple days. I wanted to see if I could talk him into looking for them scalawags."

"Blasted shame," Pappy muttered. "How many did you lose altogether?"

"Fifteen, maybe twenty head."

Pappy shook his head. "Looks like I might have to go looking for credit before long."

"Your credit's always good here, Hank."

The old rancher smiled gratefully, his wrinkled face looking like plowed ground. "Obliged, Pappy. If things don't get better, I might have to sell out like old Joe Windham."

Josh interrupted. "Pappy, I'm taking McCool's sorrel over to the saloon. I'll go inside and tell him she's ready."

Pappy winked at Hank and replied. "Better hurry, Son. Mary Simmons is like to be along right directly. You don't want to miss her." He cackled, and despite his own problems, Hank Bartholomew joined in the laughter.

The two watched Josh lead the sorrel across the street. "That cowpoke there is the best hand I ever see'd with horses."

Bartholomew arched an eyebrow. "Don't say."

"You bet your last cent. Why, he's got a knack that's just like magic." He shook his head. "Hope he stays around hereabouts."

McCool's Emporium wore a fresh coat of white-wash. From talk Josh had heard about town, Slick McCool was buying up land out east and north of Junction Flats. The whole town speculated about his intent, but all Josh had heard was gossip, and he always figured anyone who put any stock in gossip had about as much horse sense as a lovesick cowboy.

After tying the sorrel next to a big gray at the hitching rail, he ambled inside, searching the brightly lit saloon for McCool.

Though mid-morning, several cowpokes lounged about the saloon, some at tables dealing stud poker, others leaning over the bar, nursing mugs of beer or tumblers of tarantula juice straight from the wooden barrel. He spotted the dapper owner seated at a table by himself at the rear of the room. McCool saw Josh and waved him over.

Halfway down the bar, two drunken cowpokes were arguing with the bartender. "Look, boys," the rotund bartender said pleasantly. "Why don't you go home and sleep it off? Come back tomorrow. I'll give you a free drink."

Josh jerked to a halt as one jumped back and shouted. "Like blazes I'll go home." He spun around and grabbed a chair. "Nobody tells me what to do. I'll show you," he screamed, hauling back with the chair and aiming at the mirror behind the bar.

In one quick step, Josh stepped forward, grabbed the straight back chair from the surprised cowboy's hands and shattered the chair across the cowpoke's head. The cowboy dropped like a sack of flour.

"You can't do that," his partner shouted, slapping for his six-gun. The unlucky jasper never cleared leather before Josh caught him upside the head with the leg of the chair.

Tossing the leg on the floor, Josh said to the bartender. "Sheriff's out of town, I hear. You might want to haul these boys over to the jail and let them sleep it off."

"That was mighty good work, Josh," said Slick McCool coming to his side and staring down impassively at the two unconscious punchers.

"Nothing hard about handling drunks," the lanky cowboy replied. He changed the subject. "Your pony's outside at the rail like you wanted, McCool."

"Thanks." The dapper saloon owner slipped his slender fingers into his vest pocket. "Here, let me give you something." He nodded to the figures on the floor. "You earned it. Saved me the expense of a new mirror."

"No, thanks. I never cared much for them that can't hold their liquor."

A wry smile split McCool's card thin face. He flipped a gold eagle in the air. "Then here's a tip for bringing my pony to me. You don't object to that do you?"

Arching an eyebrow at the ten-dollar gold piece in his hand, Josh replied. "Not if you don't object to tipping too much."

Both men laughed.

At that moment, the batwing doors slammed open. Sonora Fats and Grat Plummer stood motionless. When Fats spotted McCool, he started toward the gambler with Grat right on his heels. Fats nodded to the saloon owner. "Here I am, McCool. What's so important?"

Nodding to the two disreputable looking owlhoots, Josh said, "Looks like you got company." He dropped the gold piece into his vest pocket. "Thanks for the tip."

A dry smile on his thin lips, McCool nodded. "Anytime."

At the door, Josh paused and glanced back, seeing McCool motioning the two hombres to follow him to his table at the rear of the saloon.

Josh couldn't help wondering about McCool and his connection with Sonora Fats. After all, he told himself. A jasper sleeps with dogs, reckon he'll catch fleas. And he supposed there was probably a heap of fleas living with Sonora Fats and his hardcases.

Back at the livery, Hank Bartholomew had departed. Pappy sat at the pot-bellied stove in the middle of the stall. With a grin, he nodded to the chair beside him on which sat a plate covered with a red and white plaid napkin. "You had a visitor. She said tell you she's sorry she missed you, but hope you like her fried chicken." He licked his fingers. "Hope you don't mind, but I et me a piece. It was right good."

Next morning after breakfast, Sheriff August Rabb showed up at the livery. He was picking his teeth and rubbing his large belly. "Hear you stopped some trouble over at McCool's yesterday, Mr. Barkley." The tips of his handlebar mustache bounced when he spoke.

"Nothing much to it," Josh replied, shoving his John B to the back of his head and wiping at the perspiration on his forehead.

"Maybe not, but I got me an offer for you. I know you was planning on moving on."

"Yeah," Josh replied, thinking of Mary Simmons. "Soon," he added.

"I hope not before you hear what I got to say."

"Shoot."

"Fact is, Mr. Barkley. I want you to come to work for me as my deputy."

For a moment, Josh stared at the sheriff, uncertain if his ears were playing tricks on him. "Did I hear you right, Sheriff?"

"I didn't stutter."

He shook his head. "I'm no lawman."

Sheriff Rabb guffawed. "Blazes, a lawman's just a regular jasper who cottons to the idea that all folks should be able to live the way they want without no one taking advantage of them." His blue eyes fixed on Josh, he stroked his mustache. "Pay's sixty a month and a room over at the Cattleman's Hotel."

Sixty a month? Twice what he was making at the livery or what he could make punching cows. "That's a heap of money for a deputy."

Rabb twirled one end of his handlebar mustache around his index finger. "You'll earn it. We've had a rash of rustling hereabouts. Not in my county, but I got a mind to look into it anyways." He hesitated, rubbing the back of his neck with a grizzled hand. "I ain't certain." His eyes narrowed. "I got a feeling a heap more is taking place than I can see. I need a good man. You'll earn your pay, don't worry."

Pappy hobbled in from the back corral. "Howdy, Sheriff. How was the trip over to Squaw Creek?"

"Good. Finished up early and rode back in late last night. Got to head back in a couple days." He nodded to Josh. "I'm trying to steal your hired hand here, Pappy. I need a deputy."

"Lordy, lordy," Pappy growled. "Don't that beat all. Get me a good hand, and then the law hires him away. You just ain't got no heart, August Rabb."

The sheriff winked at Josh. "Well? What do you say? This could be a chance to settle down and stop drifting."

Josh chuckled. "Like I say the other day, Sheriff. I like drifting."

The older man eyed Josh shrewdly. "Everyone needs a place he can call home. That's the nature of man." He paused, then added. "Unless there's some reason he can't afford to settle down."

Josh stiffened imperceptibly. He forced a crooked smile. "Sounds to me you're talking about someone on the run from the law, Sheriff."

For several moments, Sheriff Rabb studied Josh, his icy blue gaze trying to read the younger man's thoughts. "Reckon I could be talking about that, Mr. Barkley."

Josh studied the sheriff. Braxton Bragg's retreat to Ringgold, Georgia, was a year and a thousand miles past. Josh had spent a year trying to convince himself that he had done his part for the South, that he was justified in seeking a life of his own, of settling down. Maybe this was his chance. Maybe now he could still his nagging conscience. "I still have my partner, Mike Gray-Eyes."

Rabb shrugged. "Well, reckon that is a problem as far as the hotel. They sure ain't going to put up no redstick."

Pappy chimed up. "This Injun friend of yours. He good with horses? Good as you?"

"Better."

Pappy eyed Sheriff Rabb defiantly then turned to Josh. "If he wants your job here, he's got it, and the two of you can stay in the loft."

Chapter Six

Mike Gray-Eyes refused Pappy's offer, preferring to remain as far away from the white race as possible. When Slick McCool learned of the old Indian's refusal, he offered Josh and the old Kickapoo a small shack on a piece of property he owned just beyond the outskirts of Junction Flats. "Call it a small payment toward the help you gave me the other day, deputy. Besides," he added with a sly grin, "we can't have our law sleeping in makeshift camps outside of town, now can we?"

Back at camp that night, Josh gave Mike a hard look. "You figure on turning this offer down too?"

With a suspicious gleam in his eye, the irascible old Indian grunted. "When white man give Indian gift, he want more back."

Shaking his head in frustration, Josh groaned. "Well,

I'm taking McCool's offer. And like it or not, you're going with me. Winter's coming on, and your busted up old bones can't tolerate the cold like they used to. We'll stay warm and snug until spring, and then—" He hesitated. He was going to say that come spring, they'd move on down to San Antone in time to latch on to a trail herd up north.

Mike Gray-Eyes lifted an eyebrow at Josh's unfinished comment.

"And then . . . well, we'll see."

The next couple days were uneventful with the exception of Mary Simmons' daily routine of providing noon dinner for Josh, a practice of which the entire town had become aware and viewed the deputy's obvious discomfort with amusement.

More than once, Josh bristled at the light-hearted remarks about how the young woman was searching for a husband; how her Pa was looking to pawn her off on some unsuspecting jasper; how her brothers were anxious to get shed of her.

Of course, Josh realized the joking was all in fun, but more than once, his temper flared, and he snorted. "Old Archer will have to look somewheres else besides me."

Wednesday morning, Sheriff Rabb set out for Squaw Creek. Before he left, he turned to Josh. "Go talk to old Luddy over at the general store."

"Ludwig? You mean Ludwig Protkin?"

"Yep. He sent word someone had been prowling

around his place during the night. This ain't the first time the old man's imagination run away with him. Go listen to him. Make him feel better. You hear? And no need to hurry. Just sometime today."

Josh grinned. "Whatever you say, sheriff." He smiled to himself. Paying a visit to the old merchant around noon would give him a perfect excuse to be out of the jail when Mary dropped by with his dinner.

A few hours later, Josh peered out the jailhouse window, spotting two down-at-the-heel drifters on worn-out broomtails jogging down the dusty street. He paid them little attention as they pulled up in front of Junction Flats' General Store and sat in their saddles for a moment, eyeing the whitewashed clapboard storefront.

He glanced at the Regulator clock on the sideboard beside the gun rack. Almost noon. Time to amble on over to the store like the sheriff had instructed, and, he told himself with a tinge of guilt, maybe avoid Mary Simmons. He grabbed his John B off the hat rack and tugged it down over his head.

At that moment, the door swung open, and Mary Simmons popped in, a dazzling smile on her face, her blond hair flowing over the shoulders of her red gingham dress, and a cheery lilt in her voice. "Morning, Josh. Hope you're hungry. I got a plate of venison and potatoes, fried nice and crisp."

Inwardly, he groaned. Outwardly, he smiled politely and said, "Mighty nice of you, Miss Mary. But you needn't keep doing this. I can grab a bite over to Josie's Café."

"I know," she replied brightly, unperturbed by his attempt to discourage her. "But, you know how that café food is. Why, there's even talk of something called ptomaine poisoning going around from cafés. Not Josie's of course," she hastily added. "But some." She paused, finally noticing he was preparing to leave the office. "Oh, I'm so sorry. Did I interrupt something? Were you going out?"

Seeing the opportunity to escape from her, Josh nodded toward the general store. "The sheriff wanted me to pay Luddy a visit. Something about prowlers the last few nights. Reckon I best get over there." Trying not to appear too eager, he reached for the covered plate. "Here let me put this on the stove to stay warm. I'll dig in soon as I get back."

"That's perfect," she exclaimed, handing him the plate. "That's why I came early today. I was heading to the store too. We can walk over there together."

Josh bit his tongue and opened the door. "After you."

Ludwig Protkin smiled obsequiously as he slipped the last of the canned goods into the cloth bag and handed it to the grim-faced matron glaring at him from across the counter. "Here's your goods, Missus Vhite. T'ank you for your business. Tell Mister Vhite hallo for me, pleaz."

Shrugging her ample shoulders, Georgia White shot an annoyed glance at the groceries in her bag then fixed her small eyes on him. "I'll have you know that your prices are outrageous, Mr. Protkin," she snapped. "If there was another store in Junction Flats, I'd shop there."

His smile faded. He shrugged and dropped his gaze to the countertop, holding out his arms in a gesture of helplessness. "*Ja. Ich weiß.* Yes, I know, but a simple man like me—I can do nothing about prizs, Missus Vhite. It's the company I buy from what make prizs go up." He tried to appear abject, but beneath the often-used veneer of wretched servility, of ingratiating flattery, he wished the old bat would leave so he could attend the other customers in the store, especially the two cowboys eyeing the new Henry repeating rifles in his gun rack. The third customer was only Ramon Morales, a local Mex who could wait for his usual bag of flour.

To his relief, Mrs. Georgia White grunted, turned on her heel, and waddled angrily from the store, muttering unintelligibly. The slight merchant headed toward the two cowpokes, his shrewd mind was already calculating the profit if he could sell two of the Henrys.

Glancing over his shoulder at her retreating back, Ludwig Protkin smiled to himself. He had made a nice little profit off Georgia White. He turned his attention to the two unkempt cowpokes studying the Henrys. Now, it was time to make an even better profit off these two, he told himself as he quickly sized them up from their rundown boot heels to their battered floppy hats.

Rubbing his hands in anticipation, he approached the

two. One was sighting down the barrel of the Henry rifle at a barn lantern dangling from a peg on the wall. "*Gute* mornin', gentlemen. Can I halp you?"

The first cowpoke glanced around the store. "Yeah. You can," he growled, a cruel grin curling his thin lips. "You can give us all of your cash."

Chapter Seven

The slight grocery merchant jerked to a halt, his face frozen in stunned surprise.

"And we mean now," whispered the second hardcase as he swung the muzzle of the Henry directly between Ludwig's eyes.

Bewildered by the brazen holdup in midday, the diminutive merchant stammered, but no words came out. The first holdup man spun Ludwig around and shoved him toward the counter. "Get over there and open that drawer if you don't want to buy six feet of dirt." Over his shoulder, he called out to his partner. "Keep an eye on that Mex."

"Don't fret about me," the second owlhoot replied, grabbing a box of rimfire .44 cartridges for the Henry. He pointed the Henry at the old Mexican. "You. Old man. Get over next to the counter."

The first one called over his shoulder. "Keep an eye outside too. Anybody comes in, you know what to do."

"Don't worry about me. Just get the cash."

Unaware of the holdup in the general store, Mary and Josh strolled leisurely along the boardwalk. The bright-eyed little blond hung on to Josh's arm and kept up an animated conversation. The young deputy responded with short, but polite answers. Once or twice, he caught a glimpse of a grinning face as they passed a building.

She squeezed his arm. "The church is planning on a box dinner next week to raise money for books for the school. Have you heard about it?"

He nodded, keeping his eyes fixed forward. "Seems like."

"Box dinners are always so much fun. I plan on fried chicken and apple cobbler or chocolate cake. Do you like chocolate cake or apple cobbler better?"

He shrugged. "I like 'em both."

"And," she added, lowering her voice conspiratorially. "I'm going to tie a bright yellow ribbon around my box."

At that moment, Hank Bartholomew stepped out of the Wells Fargo and almost collided with the two. He jerked back and apologized.

Josh grinned. "My fault, Hank. Sorry."

The old rancher nodded and spoke to Mary. "Hear your Pa's sending a herd down to Kerrville."

The young blond nodded energetically. "A hundred

head. The boys are pulling out first thing in the morning, Mr. Bartholomew."

"Kinda late in the year, ain't it?"

She shrugged. "I suppose, but Pa says we need some cash to get us through the winter." She hesitated, then added, "Of course, I don't need to tell you how hard things have been."

The old rancher chuckled wryly. "Sure don't. Your Pa going?"

Josh's eyes were drawn to movement through the windows of the general store next door. He spotted a stranger shoving the little German merchant across the room. Before Mary could reply to Bartholomew's question, Josh pushed her into the old rancher's arms. "Take her, Hank. Get her back inside. Quick."

Mary gasped. Bartholomew called out, "What's going on?"

Dropping into a crouch and scooting beneath the windows of the general store, Josh unleathered his .36 Navy Colt and waved behind his back at Hank and Mary, indicating for them to stay put.

Just before he reached the door, he pressed up against the clapboard wall between the door and window. He glanced back at the Wells Fargo office. Hank and Mary stood in the middle of the boardwalk, staring at him, baffled by his actions. He waved them inside, but they ignored him.

He muttered a curse under his breath. Of all the hardheaded, contrary . . . Footsteps echoing off the puncheon floors from inside cut off his angry reproach of the two. Josh flexed his fingers on the butt of his Colt. He figured at least two owlhoots, probably the drifters he had spotted riding into town only minutes earlier.

Suddenly, the door jerked open and the muzzle of a rifle appeared. Josh grabbed the muzzle and yanked, jerking the surprised hardcase outside and ripping the Henry from the startled outlaw's hands.

"What the—"

Instantly, Josh jabbed the butt of the Henry in the owlhoot's belly, and when the befuddled cowpoke doubled over, Josh slammed the muzzle of his six-gun on the back of the gunnie's head.

"Josh!" He spun at Mary's scream and came face to face with the second owlhoot. Instantly he tossed the rifle at the hombre, who grabbed at it in surprise.

The leathery deputy leaped at the startled outlaw, driving him back into the store and grabbing the hand holding the six-gun. His own gun hand slammed against the doorjamb, knocking the Colt from his fingers.

Rage twisted the heavily bearded face of the robber. He tried to fight back, to reverse the momentum of Josh's charge, but his feet tangled, and he went down on his back, banging his head on the floor sharply. His gun flew from his hand when Josh landed on top of him.

The breath whooshed from the drifter, and his body went limp.

Staggering back outside, Josh grabbed the outlaw sprawled on the porch and jerked him to his feet. The jasper came up swinging and cursing, catching Josh on the point of the chin and slamming him against a post supporting the porch. The young deputy's head bounced off the post. He lunged forward, throwing a straight right, then following it with a left hook to the jaw.

The grizzled owlhoot facing him shrugged off the blow and rocked Josh with a roundhouse right. Stars exploded in his head, but he clenched his teeth and waded into the larger hombre, pounding his knotted fists into the heavier hombre's belly.

Suddenly, Mary's scream of rage cut through the roaring in Josh's ears and his opponent lurched forward with a startled curse on his lips. "What the—"

He began spinning, and that's when Josh spotted Mary Simmons clinging to the jasper's back like a leech, her arms circling his neck, and her legs around his waist.

Josh grabbed at her as she spun past, but missed.

The outlaw was grabbing over the back of his head for the little demon clawing and screaming at him. Fearful of hitting Mary, Josh refused to take a punch at the outlaw whose defense was down.

Finally, he grabbed Mary and yanked her off. "You're going to get yourself killed. Now stay out of this!"

A thick fist slammed into the back of his head, knocking him to the boardwalk. He hit and rolled just as a boot heel smashed into the wood beside his head. He kicked at the jasper's other leg and sent him tumbling to the boardwalk.

Instantly, the owlhoot leaped to his feet, and Josh met him, arms pumping, fists pounding.

Without warning, Josh's head exploded, and a great blackness engulfed him.

When Josh opened his eyes, all he could see was a blur of faces. Then he recognized Mary who was kneeling at his side, washing his face with a cool rag. Behind her, the faces came into focus, and he recognized Hank Bartholomew, Luddy Protkin, and the postmaster, Lester Boles.

"What—what happened? Did they get away?"

Bartholomew grinned. "Them two's over in jail. Lester and me just now put'em there."

Josh frowned. "How—I mean . . . I don't understand. One of them knocked me out, didn't he?"

No one replied. Mary's face turned crimson. She mumbled. "Well, Josh. Not exactly."

Not exactly? He closed his eyes, trying to clear his head. "What do you mean, not exactly?"

Hank Bartholomew chuckled. "Reckon you best tell him, Mary. If you gotta eat crow, it's best to do it while it's warm."

She shot the old rancher a fiery look. "If it's anything I don't need now, Mr. Bartholomew, it's any of your old folk sayings."

Josh focused his eyes on Mary. She was chewing on her lip and looked like she wanted to cry. "What's he talking about? And how did those two jaspers get in jail?"

She cleared her throat. "Well, you see, Josh, here's what happened. After you pulled me off that . . . that

hateful creature, I—well, I wanted to help you, so—"
She hesitated.

"Go on, Mary." Luddy Protkin urged her with a grin.
"Get it over vith."

"I am, I am. Just give me time."

"Keep putting it off, Mary, and it'll never get done,"
drawled the old rancher in amusement.

She set her jaw, and her eyes blazed up at the grinning faces about her. "All right, I will." She turned back
to the prone deputy. "Here's what happened, Josh.
After you pulled me off him, I was afraid he'd hurt you
so, so I grabbed the rifle and tried to hit him."

Suddenly, the clouds parted, and Josh understood.
"And instead of hitting him, you cold-cocked me."

The young blond dropped her gaze and nodded slowly, her face filled with anguish. "I didn't mean to hit
you, Josh. Honest. I just wanted to help. He was bigger
than you. I was afraid he'd hurt you something bad. I'm
sorry. I'm so sorry."

Josh stared up at her. Behind her bowed head, the
audience was grinning from ear to ear. He looked back
her. How could he be angry? She was just trying to
help—much to his own misfortune.

He cleared his throat. "Don't worry yourself about it,
Miss Mary. I've always had a head harder than rock
granite. I'm just mighty obliged for you trying to help."

She smiled at him gratefully. "So, you're not mad at
me?"

"No." He struggled to sit up, wincing as the sudden

movement sent shards of pain through his skull. He closed his eyes tightly, waiting for the pain to subside. "But, how did those jaspers end up in jail if I was unconscious? You do it, Hank, Lester?"

The grin on Bartholomew's face grew broader. "Ask her. She did it."

"Huh?" Josh frowned.

"That's right," Luddy said.

Lester Boles chimed in. "Never seen nothing like it, Deputy. After she cold-cocked you, that other jasper just stood staring down at you in surprise, so this little filly promptly whopped him upside the head with the Henry rifle. Look at the knot on the side of his head when you get the chance. She put it there."

All Josh could do was stare at Mary Simmons in disbelief. He finally found his voice. "You did that? You really did that?"

She nodded slowly.

"Lordy, lordy," he muttered. He clambered to his feet unsteadily. "That is truly something, Miss Mary. I'm mighty indebted to you."

Her face brightened, and her eyes lit up. "Really?"

Josh forced a grin. "Really."

"You sure you're not mad at me?"

Behind her, Hank and Lester grinned like possums. Josh shrugged uncomfortably. "Yes, Ma'am, I'm sure. I'm not mad at you."

"You're really, really certain you're not mad at me?"

"No, Ma'am. Honest."

Her face beamed. "Does that mean you'll buy my box at the church's box dinner then?"

All the young deputy could do was stare at her, a tiny woman with the nerve and gall of a giant. "Well, yes, ma'am. I reckon it does."

Chapter Eight

With Hank Bartholomew and Mary on either side of the addled deputy, Josh stumbled unsteadily back to the jail to check on his prisoners and maybe grab a short nap to perhaps ease the pain in his throbbing head.

"Need any help?"

Josh glanced around at the shout.

Dressed in his usual dark dovetail jacket and gray trousers, Slick McCool stood on the edge of the boardwalk in front of his saloon. Grat Plummer and Sonora Fats slouched on either side of him.

"Reckon not," Bartholomew shouted back. "He's just a little groggy. He'll be all right when he gets some rest."

McCool hooked his thumbs in the pockets of his

checkered vest and nodded. "Let me know if he needs anything."

Behind him, a sly grin spread over Sonora Fat's thick lips. The sheriff was out of town over to Squaw Creek and now the deputy was addled.

"Well, McCool. Reckon we'll ride." He dipped his head. "Obliged." He nudged Grat with his elbow. "Let's hit the leather."

From inside the Community Methodist Church, Reverend Matthew Adams peered through the window, squinting as he watched his older brother and his no-good sidekick, Grat Plummer, nod to McCool, climb into their saddles, and ride north out of town in the direction of the Simmons' ranch. A faint smile ticked up his lips. Maybe his brother had taken his suggestion and was heading out to the Simmons' to hire on for the cattle drive the old man was taking down to Kerrville.

Maybe Elmer was going to change. Maybe—

"Blast," the preacher muttered when he spotted Lester Boles, the postmaster, step outside the post office and glance nervously around before moving his bay horse from north end of the hitching rail to the south, their prearranged signal for an immediate meeting. Adams' exasperation with the timid little man's nagging worries was growing, worries the preacher told himself, usually over nothing more than imaginary fears.

He had met Boles two years earlier in the riverfront saloons in St. Louis where he had fled after deserting the Third Texas Cavalry in Shreveport. Boles introduced him to Union sympathizers, and when approached by an agent of the commander of the military district of Kansas, he agreed to return to Texas as a federal spy—as soon as five thousand dollars was deposited in his personal account at the bank in St. Louis, plus a cut of every shipment of Confederate gold he managed to get into Union hands.

Boles had already been entrenched in Junction Flats, and for the last several months, the two had worked together providing Union sympathizers with information on Southern troop movements.

Recently, word had filtered out that the Confederacy was planning a large gold shipment. As soon as details were available, Reverend Adams would pay a visit to Lee Rohmann, a conspirators who lived out on Viejo Creek, who in turn would initiate the plot to steal the gold with the aid of the local Copperheads.

Usually meetings between the preacher and Boles were shrouded under the cover of darkness. For the small man to call one in the middle of the day suggested urgency. The reverend guessed the nervous postmaster must have received news concerning the shipment and that was the reason for the meeting.

Straightening his severely fitting black coat and tugging his plain black hat down on his head, the Reverend Matthew Adams crossed the street to the post office.

On the road north of town, Sonora Fats shouted above the pounding of hoofbeats. "You get ahold of Rowdy and Selman?"

The hatchet faced man riding at Fats' side grunted. "They're meeting us at the fork. Bringing two more like you said. Where do you reckon the herd is about now?"

"We got time. We'll spend the night at the old fort, then hit the herd tomorrow at Devil's Butte. That's outside of Kimble County. That way, we keep out of Sheriff Rabb's business."

Grat nodded, glancing through narrowed eyes at his boss. Fats was a puzzle to the cold-blooded killer. He was always visiting the preacher—Adams. Made no sense, the owlhoot told himself. None at all. And the few times he had broached the subject, Sonora Fats told him in no uncertain terms it was none of his business.

Next morning, Josh still wore a knot, but the pounding had subsided. Just after noontime, as Josh sat cleaning his Navy Colt, Sheriff Rabb rode in from Squaw Creek and listened with amusement as Josh related the events of the previous day.

"Whopped you upside the head, you say?" He grinned like a fox eyeing the henhouse.

Josh touched the knot on the back of his head gingerly. With a wry grin, he replied. "Yes, Sir. And as hard as she could."

The sheriff glanced up at the Regulator clock. He grunted. "It's one o'clock. She ain't showed up with your dinner. Reckon she's too embarrassed about whopping you to show her face?"

"I doubt that," Josh replied, lifting an eyebrow.

"From what I've seen of Miss Mary, there isn't much of anything that would embarrass her." He cut his eyes toward the clock. She was late. Maybe with the cattle drive starting out for Kerrville, she had enough on her hands to keep her busy.

Sheriff Rabb chuckled. "If I didn't know better," he joked. "I'd figure that little filly was making you nervous."

Pausing while ramming the cleaning rag down the barrel of his Navy Colt, Josh glanced at the sheriff, spotting the laughter in the older man's eyes. "Go ahead. Laugh, but that young lady's got marriage on her mind."

"Well," the sheriff replied, pulling out a bag of Bull Durham and building a cigarette. "Reckon she might, but she's mighty handsome, and her Pa's got a nice spread."

"Maybe so," Josh retorted, jamming his Colt back in its holster. "But that don't interest me at all. No, sir, not one iota. And don't go thinking she won't be back. She will."

Before Sheriff Rabb could reply, the door burst open and Mary Simmons rushed in. Her face was flushed, and her blond hair tangled from a hard ride. "Sheriff, Josh, come quick! Rustlers stole the herd and shot up Ed real bad. Doc Sears is already on the way out to the ranch."

Chapter Nine

Archer Simmons sat slumped forward in a straight back chair, his elbows on the dining room table, his face buried in his hands. Kelt and Ham sat across the table, staring grim-faced at the closed door behind which Doc Sears worked on the youngest brother. Mary was inside assisting the doctor.

Josh stood just inside the door as Sheriff Rabb sat beside the distraught old rancher. The sheriff laid his hand on Archer's shoulder. "The boy'll make it, Arch. He's tough."

The old man's shoulders shuddered. "Ain't nobody tougher than lead slugs, August John."

His voice growing lighter, the sheriff replied, "Can't deny that, but stubborn helps too, and one thing about the Simmons' clan, they're stubborn."

Ham chuckled, a grin breaking the hard lines of his face. "He ain't lying about that, Pa."

Archer Simmons shook his head. "Lord. I ain't much of a host today, August John. Sorry. Kelt, pour the sheriff and the deputy some coffee. Reckon I could use some too."

The sheriff grunted. "Coffee would taste right good, Arch. Obliged."

As Kelt poured steaming coffee into thick mugs, the sheriff asked. "How many was out there, Kelt?"

"Can't really say." He paused in pouring the coffee and glanced at his brother. "They hit us when we pushed the herd between Devil's Butte and Viejo Creek. Never saw hide nor hair of them."

"That's right, Sheriff," Ham chimed in. "They was up on the butte and hid out in the underbrush along the creek. From the lead they was throwing at us, I'd say six or seven."

Kelt filled Josh's cup. "Hard to say just how many." He hesitated and glanced at the closed door. His voice cracked. "Ed—Ed went down right off. The herd stampeded." The young cowpoke chewed on his bottom lip, locking eyes with his brother.

Ham looked around at his Pa. "I hate we lost the herd, Pa, but it was Ed we was worried about."

Archer Simmons grunted and forced a grin. "Boys, I'd of tromped your britches good if you hadn't. We can always get more cows. I can't get another son." He turned his weary eyes back to the sheriff. "You going to look for them?"

The sheriff glanced up at Josh, then gave the old rancher an uncomfortable look. "You know as well as me, Arch, Devil's Butte is out in No-Mans Land. There ain't no law out there to give us a hand. Legally, my jurisdiction ends on the west border of Kimble County." He hesitated. "But, Josh and me, we'll ride out and see where the trail leads. A herd that size won't be hard to follow."

Ham cleared his throat. "Not if they head to the trace. You know what happens to the rustled herds that go out there to the trace."

The sheriff glanced at Josh, noting the puzzled expression on his deputy's face. He explained. "What Ham's talking about is how several rustled herds have been tracked to the old buffalo trace only to disappear."

Josh chuckled in disbelief. "Disappear? How can a herd disappear?"

"That's what no one has figured out," Ham replied. "The sign's there one minute, the next it's gone."

Sheriff Rabb nodded to Josh. "Like ghosts."

"Except there's no such thing as ghosts," Josh answered.

"Maybe not, Josh," Kelt added. "But sometimes I've wondered if that's about the only explanation there can be."

The sheriff cleared his throat. "Don't worry, Arch. If they come back into Kimble County, I'll nab them."

"If they don't?"

Rabb looked around into the hard eyes of Kelt Simmons. "We can go after them out of Kimble County, but the law won't be with us."

Kelt nodded, a faint grin twisting his lips. "That's just fine with me. I don't care much about the law being around when I catch up with them what shot up my little brother."

"Me neither," Hamm said.

His face reflecting the mixed feelings tumbling through his head, Sheriff Rabb pushed back from the table and looked down at the old rancher. "Arch. I'll try to find them that did this, but I got to level with you right now. I been a lawman all my life. We catch them, I'll bring them back for trial. There ain't going to be no vigilante justice with me around."

Archer Simmons looked up into the sheriff's icy blue eyes. For several seconds, the two old friends studied each other. Finally, Archer nodded. "The boys'll go with you, August John." He glared at his sons, issuing a stern warning. "They'll do exactly what you say."

"Good enough." Sheriff Rabb slapped his six-gun. "It's late, Archer. Josh and me'll ride back into town and pick up our gear. We'll be back before first light. You boys be ready to ride out, you hear?"

Ham and Kelt nodded as their Pa replied, "Don't worry, August John. They'll be ready."

Throughout the day, Sonora Fats drove his men and the rustled herd west until they hit the broad trace cut out over the centuries by great herds of migrating buffalo. There, they followed the trace south, from time to time as their routine, cutting fifteen or so beeves from the main herd and sending one puncher to drive them

west to a box canyon miles beyond the abandoned and
crumbling Fort Terrett in that forbidding desolation
civilization called No-Man's Land.

Whittling down the stolen herd in such a manner was
a common maneuver Sonora Fats followed to eventual-
ly erase all sign. More than once, he had duped and
deceived trackers who clung to the trail, tenaciously
following the sign only to discover miles down the
trace, all fresh sign had suddenly vanished. He grunted, and a crooked grin played over his round face. He
was constantly amazed that none of the trackers had
figured out just how he carried off the deception. "So
dumb they couldn't find a cow-bell in their own bed,"
he muttered.

By dusk, Fats drifted the last of the beeves off the
trace onto rocky ground covered with sparse wiry
bunchgrass. He glanced at the first stars glittering in the
western sky, promising a clear and bright night. By
midnight, he would have the last of the herd in the
canyon.

Josh and the sheriff held their ponies in a mile-eating
walking two-step. "Been much rustling around hereabouts, Sheriff?"

"Not in my county, but other counties around here
have had a heap. Menard, Edwards, Mason."

A frown wrinkled Josh's forehead. "Why them and
not your county?"

The starlight painted the crooked grin on Sheriff
Rabb's lips with a bluish glow. "Me. I ain't accusing
the law around us of nothing, but owlhoots know if they

sneeze out of place in my county, I'll come down on them with both boot heels. Why—"

Suddenly, the chilling buzz of rattles cut into the sheriff's words. Josh's pony shied, almost spilling the lanky cowpoke from the saddle while the Sheriff Rabb's horse reared, pawing at the stars and unseating the surprised sheriff.

Instantly, Josh shucked his .36 caliber Colt and in the blink of an eye, put two slugs in the shadowy coils of the fat rattlesnake in the middle of the dusty road, the second of which tore off the sidewinder's spade-shaped head.

He wheeled Buck around. "Sheriff! You all right?"

A string of curses erupted from the groaning shadow on the ground. "No, I ain't all right. I busted my blasted leg," he growled between clenched teeth.

Josh dismounted quickly. The sheriff's right leg was twisted at a grotesque angle under him. "Lay back, Sheriff," he said, placing a hand on Rabb's shoulder. "Let me see what I can do."

"Ain't nothing you can do." The strained words burst out between gritted teeth. He lay back and closed his eyes. "You're going to have to straighten it out, Josh. Yank the no-good traitor straight and set it best you can."

Glancing around, Josh spotted a broken branch. He snapped off a short length and stuck it between the sheriff's teeth. "Here. Bite on this."

Rabb spit it out. "Don't tell me you're dumb enough to believe that old wives' tale. It's going to hurt like sin one way or another. Just get started and don't stop no matter how much I cuss, you hear?"

"All right, Sheriff. Get ready. I'm going to straighten it."

The sheriff took a deep breath. "Then stop jawing and do it."

Gently, Josh began straightening the twisted leg.

A scream of pain burst from the sheriff's lips. "Darn it, don't dawdle. Straighten the blasted thing!"

Josh hesitated, looking up into the sheriff's face anxiously. "It'll hurt like sin."

"Then do it!" Fists clenched, his body taut as a coiled spring, the sheriff clenched his teeth against the pain.

Without warning, Josh yanked the leg straight.

A strangled groan escaped from the sheriff's throat, and he fainted.

Josh worked quickly, feeling along the leg, hoping the bones were where they should be. He had set legs before, twice during the war.

Chopping a couple branches from a mesquite with his sheath knife, he fashioned splints, then snugged them down with the sheriff's lariat until the leg from knee to ankle was encased in coils of rope.

Sitting back on his haunches, Josh stared at the sweat-covered face of the unconscious sheriff. "Now, all I got to do is figure how to get you on back to town."

In answer to his question, the rattling of Doc Sears' surrey broke the silence of the night.

* * *

Twenty minutes later, the two laid the still unconscious sheriff on a bunk in the doctor's office. "When he wakes up, Doc. Tell him I'm out looking for the rustlers' trail."

Chapter Ten

The early morning was unseasonably warm for late October. The breeze came from out of the southeast, carrying with it a warm flow off the Gulf of Mexico.

Josh and Mike Gray-Eyes rode up to the Simmons' house just after four. A lantern appeared in the door, and Archer Simmons stepped out on the porch, holding the lantern high. His craggy face twisted into a puzzled frown.

Josh quickly explained about the sheriff and announced that he and Mike Gray-Eyes were going after the herd.

The older brother, Kelt, stepped into the lantern light, his jaw set rock-hard. He growled belligerently. "I ain't riding with no redstick."

With an indifferent shrug, Josh replied. "Up to you,

Kelt. You can go with us or by yourself . . . or stay here."

"Do what you want. I'm going with them," a voice said, and Mary Simmons stepped into the light. She was dressed for riding and patted the saddlebags draped over her arm. "I got grub here for a couple days."

Hamm blurted out. "No, you ain't. You're staying here, girl. And that's final."

Fire blazed in her eyes. She spun on her older brother. "You don't tell me what to do, Hammond Frank Simmons. I'm a grown woman, and I'll do what I blasted well choose to do."

Their Pa broke it up. "Both of you hush up." He glared at Ham and Kelt. "This ain't the time to argue none about redsticks. You know how important that herd is to the ranch. Now, I don't want to hear no more arguing." He looked down at Mary. "You be careful, you hear?"

She smiled reassuringly. "Don't worry, Pa." She shot a devastating glare at her brothers. "You know I can outride and outshoot either of those two."

"All right then. Saddle up." He looked up at Josh. "Want some coffee while the kids saddle their ponies?"

Josh glanced at the old Kickapoo who was staring unseeing at the lantern in the rancher's hand. "Appreciate it, but I'll wait out here."

Arch cut his eyes to the old Indian, then quickly back to Josh. "Your choice."

"How's Ed doing this morning?"

"About as well as could be expected. Looks like there might be a little infection, but we been doctoring it. The wounds are seeping a lot." He shook his head. "Can't tell if what Doc Sears gave is helping or not."

"Infection?" Josh glanced at Mike Gray-Eyes who continued to stare impassively at the lantern in Arch's hand. He turned back to the old rancher. "Mr. Simmons, you can say no, and it won't hurt our feelings, but Mike Gray-Eyes here was a medicine man in his tribe before they run him out to die. I've seen him mix up concoctions for everything from dropsy to headache, and they all worked. He can probably whip up something for infection if you got a mind to try it."

Archer Simmons hesitated. He glanced over his shoulder in the direction of his son's bedroom, then up at the old Indian. Josh saw the confusion on the old rancher's face and knew he was arguing with himself. Which would win out, his son or the prejudice with which he had lived all his life?

"You say that redstic—I mean, Injun is some kind of doctor?"

"I don't know about doctor, but I've seen him make sick folks well."

The old rancher chewed on his bottom lip. "Truth is, I'd go to any lengths for my youngsters, even if they is growed up. I'd be much obliged if your friend there could help my boy."

Josh looked around at Mike. "Think you can help?"

Mike Gray-Eyes nodded.

"Will you?"

The old Indian hesitated, then nodded once again. He slipped the parfleche bag off his shoulder. "Need light."

Josh took the lantern from Archer and held it up so Mike Gray-Eyes could see as he rummaged through the parfleche bag. He retrieved two small deerskin bags and handed them to Josh. "Make salve with water. Make white eyes good."

"Here, Mr. Simmons. Do what he said. Mix these together with some water and rub them on the wounds."

The rancher took the bags warily. "You reckon it'll really work?"

"If it doesn't, throw 'em away."

Approaching hoofbeats interrupted them.

"We're ready," Mary called out.

Josh pulled his buckskin around. "Let's ride. Hamm, you and Kelt lead the way to where the rustlers hit."

Mike Gray-Eyes hesitated as a sudden gust of wind blew in from the south. He drew a deep breath as if he smelled the early morning. "Storm come."

Kelt looked up at the starry heavens and snorted. "Not likely."

Kelt took the lead, Mary and Hamm fell in behind their brother, and Josh and Mike Gray-Eyes brought up the rear. The old Indian growled under his breath. "Woman cause trouble."

Josh grinned crookedly. "Maybe so, old friend, but I

know from bitter experience that no one's going to stop her from coming with us."

Mike grunted. "Not good."

Two hours later, they reached Devil's Butte. Hamm nodded to the boulder-strewn slopes of the large mesa. "Yonder's where the shots came from. There and along the creek banks behind the cattails."

"When the shooting started, Ed went down," Kelt said. "The herd bolted south. We was both back here with Ed. The stampede stirred up so much dust, we couldn't see our horses' rumps."

The ground was churned up like a drift of razorbacks had been rooting around. "This ain't going to hard to follow," Kelt exclaimed, putting his horse into a gallop along the trail.

A mile farther, the trail cut abruptly to the right, crossed Viejo Creek and continued directly west through a rocky tableland of mesquite and stunted live oak. "A couple miles ahead of us is the old buffalo trace," Mary Simmons shouted above the pounding of hooves against the rocky soil.

Josh nodded. The trace. That was where the trail always vanished.

Abruptly, the wind switched to the north, carrying with it a sharp edge and dropping the temperature. A sidelong glance at Mike Gray-Eyes revealed nothing, not even the slightest sign of a smug 'I-told-you-so.' The old man simply tightened the neck of his buckskin shirt and tugged his hat down tighter on his head.

Ominous dark clouds rolled over the northern horizon. Ahead, Hamm reached over and nudged Kelt, indicating the clouds. Kelt shook his head and continued riding.

Minutes later, they reached the trace where the trail turned south. The trail was clear as creek water, so clear they could follow it at a gallop. Josh studied the torn up ground, noting that every quarter mile or so, thick deposits of limestone cobbles crossed the trace.

Behind, the threatening clouds raced toward them, and within a few miles, a cold rain struck, soaking them instantly as well as quickly washing out the sign of the rustled herd.

Josh shouted for the brothers to rein up. "We best find some shelter," he shouted above the roar of the wind and the pounding of the rain. "This looks like a bad storm."

"Not us," Kelt retorted. "We're staying on the trail."

"In ten minutes, there won't be a trail." He glanced up at the thick clouds rolling across the desolate countryside, pressing down on them. "We best find us a place to shelter up. The butte is only two or three miles back. If we ride hard, maybe we can reach there before the worst of the storm hits."

Hamm shook his head. "We're going on with Kelt. You and the redstick can go back, but we're going on." He reined his pony about. "Come on, Mary."

She shot Josh an uncertain glance, then shook her head. "Don't be crazy, Hamm. The rain will wash out the trail. You'll get caught out here without any shelter. You could freeze to death."

"Freeze? This is October. Nobody freezes in October."

She glared at him. "It's almost November, but you've seen snow in October just like I have. This storm looks bad."

Her brother eyed her with disgust. "Then you go on with the deputy. We're going after Pa's herd." He slammed his spurs into the pony's flanks. The startled horse leaped forward, and mud flying from its hooves, raced after Kelt.

Josh pulled beside Mary Simmons. "Sorry, Miss Mary."

"Don't be," she snorted, staring after her brothers. "Those two were always stubborner than mules." She looked up at him, turning her head into the wind so her hat would block the rain. "Now what?"

"The butte. Looks like that's the nearest shelter around."

From where they sat their ponies, the tabletop of Devil's butte was directly northeast. They headed for it, holding their head and shoulders into the biting wind and rain that seemed to be growing colder by the minute.

It was only midday, but the clouds made it seem like dusk. Just before they reached Viejo Creek, Mike Gray-Eyes reined up. "Wait!"

Mary and Josh exchanged surprised looks.

The old Indian leaned forward in his saddle and peered through the veil of rain that almost blocked out their view of the creek. Taking his crutch, he slid off his horse and ground reined it. Without a word, he limped into the storm.

"Where's he going?"

Josh shook his head. "No idea. Just wait."

Minutes later, a shadow appeared from out of the rain. Mike halted his pony and gestured to the creek with his crutch. "Comanche. Camp on creek." He made a sweeping motion with his arm to the north, then back east. "We make circle." He shook his head. "No sound." He swung into the saddle with surprising agility and headed north. "Come."

Mary frowned up at Josh. "Are you sure he knows where he's going?" The young woman whispered.

"I'd bet on it. The old man never stays in one place. He's always out wandering the countryside. Says it keeps him young."

She arched a skeptical eyebrow at him. Josh just shrugged. "That's what he says."

A few minutes later, they cut back east toward the creek. The creek bank was a small bluff. Before Mike Gray-Eyes could warn her, Mary rode up to the edge, which, soaked by the rain, abruptly caved in, carrying both her and her horse into the chilly water.

She screamed as she tumbled from the saddle.

Josh grimaced, then cut his eyes in the direction of the Comanche camp. No sense in being quiet now, he told himself, digging his heels into the buckskin's flanks and driving the startled animal into the creek. He grabbed her horse's reins while the old Indian snatched the back of Mary's jacket and dragged her across the creek, muttering loud enough for Josh to hear. "Trouble. Woman is always trouble."

"Quick. Get on," Josh shouted at Mary. She clambered to her feet, slipped in the mud and fell to her knees just as the first cries of the Comanche reached them.

Mary Simmons' eyes grew wide.

"You hear? Get in that blasted saddle. We've got to light a shuck out of here."

The old Kickapoo exclaimed once again. "Woman is always trouble." He wheeled his pinto about and slammed his moccasined heels into the animal's flanks.

In the next instant, Mary leaped to her feet and swung into the saddle. She dug her heels into her pony's flanks, sending the mare racing after Mike Gray-Eyes. Josh brought up the rear.

Coming up fast behind, the excited war whoops of half-a-dozen blood-lusting Comanche pounded in Josh's ears.

The spray of mud thrown up by Mike Gray-Eyes' and Mary's ponies stung Josh's face. He narrowed his eyes, keeping his head down and peering from under his eyebrows so the crown of his John B caught the larger chunks of mud.

He shot a glance over his shoulder. Through the heavy rain, he could make out the vague outline of the Comanche warrior in the lead.

He shucked his Colt and twisted around in the saddle. He didn't figure on hitting anything, only slowing them down. "Hope my powder's dry," he muttered, squeezing off a shot.

The powder exploded, and a balloon of smoke filled

the air. Behind, the Comanches swerved, enabling Josh to gain a few more precious feet.

He touched off three more shots, not figuring on hitting anything, but at least sending up balloons of smoke that, mingled with the driving rain, partially obscured the Comanche's vision.

Chapter Eleven

Mike Gray-Eyes swung around the north side of the butte. Josh glanced over his shoulder. The Comanches were gaining.

Racing past a stand of scrub oak, the old Kickapoo cut sharply to the right between two large boulders. Mary and Josh followed, finding themselves racing recklessly down a narrow trail that twisted and wound through house-sized boulders until they reined up out of the rain beneath an overhang of yellow limestone.

As they listened, the pounding of hoof beats passed and faded into the distance, as did the last of daylight. They sat in the darkness without moving, feeling the thudding of their hearts gradually slowing. Then the old Kickapoo dismounted. The sharp click of steel against flint broke the silence. A yellow spark leaped to a tiny pile of tinder, and a small yellow flame burst to life.

Deftly, Mike Gray-Eyes built a small torch, then kicked out the fire. "Come." He grunted as he mounted his pinto.

He led the way into a wide fissure in the rock. Josh and Mary followed.

The torchlight flickered on the walls on either side of the tunnel. The musty smell of a cave enveloped them. Soon, the sound of the storm faded, and all Josh could hear was the sharp click of iron horseshoes against the rocky floor.

Finally, the old Indian reined up. "We stay." He held the torch over his head, revealing a small cavern.

Within minutes a small fire warmed the chamber. While the coffee boiled, Mary studied Mike Gray-Eyes with new respect. "How did you find this place? I've lived around here all my life, and I had no idea it was here."

Josh grinned wryly when the old Kickapoo pointed to his eyes and replied. "White man never see. Indian see all."

She shook her head slowly. "I can believe that." Her face grew pensive. "I hope Hamm and Kelt are safe."

Josh grinned at her. "Don't worry. They can take care of themselves." From what he had seen of the two brothers, he didn't figure they had much of a chance to take care of anything, but what was a white lie if it put her at ease?

Mike Gray-Eyes stiffened, his eyes glazing over as if he were peering into another world. He rose and reached for the small torch.

Josh frowned. "Something wrong?"

"I be back," was all Mike Gray-Eyes said, leaning on his crutch and limping from the chamber.

"Where's he going?" Mary asked as the old Indian shuffled into the tunnel.

"No idea." Josh leaned forward and poured another cup of coffee. "But, like he said, he'll be back."

Ten minutes later, Mike Gray-Eyes returned, leading Hamm's horse with the young man slumped forward over the horse's neck. Kelt brought up the rear.

For a moment, Mary sat transfixed, then with a gasp of alarm, jumped to her feet and rushed to her brother. Josh helped her ease the young man to the ground. A Comanche arrow protruded from his back, fledged with three feathers extending almost a quarter of the length of the arrow shaft. The brownish gray feathers drooped from the rain.

His face pale with pain, Ham clenched his teeth and squeezed his eyes shut. Mike Gray-Eyes rolled the young cowpoke onto his side and quickly slit the young man's garments from around the wound.

Kelt grimaced and muttered a curse. The old Kickapoo ignored the young man, his ancient fingers flying deftly over the wound. He tugged gently on the shaft. "No good," he muttered, looking up at Josh. "Comanche use metal tip. It come off if we pull arrow out. It make rot inside, and he die."

Mary's face twisted in anguish. "We've got to do something."

Josh and Mike exchanged knowing looks. The deputy laid his hand on the groaning man's arm. "We got no choice, Hamm. We've got to push the arrow on through. It's going to hurt worse than you ever felt."

While he spoke Mike Gray-Eyes fumbled in his parfleche bag and pulled out a tiny clove. He diced the clove, scraped it into the cup of his hand, and held it to Hamm's lips. "Swallow. Drink water. Pain not so bad."

"What is it?" Kelt demanded, glaring suspiciously at Mike Gray-Eyes.

"Peyote," Josh replied. "I'd forgotten about that. Within a few minutes, it eases the pain away so it won't be so bad when we take out the arrow."

The flames from the small fire reflected the beads of sweat standing out on Hamm's face. Mary held out her hand to the old Indian. "Here. Give me the peyote. Kelt, get the canteen." Gently, she lifted her brother's head. "Open up."

Eyes squeezed in pain, the young man did as she said. She dumped the peyote between his parched lips and touched the mouth of the canteen to his lips. He gulped greedily, sloshing water down his throat.

"We wait now," Mike announced.

Several minutes passed. Slowly, the tremors of pain faded from Hamm's face as the peyote took effect.

Finally, the old Kickapoo said, "Roll on side."

They followed the old man's orders while he searched the chamber for a flat rock. He studied it a moment, then said, "Hold tight."

Kelt knelt by his younger brother. "Scream all you want, partner."

Hamm forced a weak grin. "You'd never let me forget that, would you?"

Kelt grinned. "Reckon I wouldn't." His fingers dug into his brother's shoulder.

Josh winked at Mary, then tightened his grip on Hamm's shoulder. He nodded to Mike. "We're ready."

Before Josh could blink an eye, the old Kickapoo slammed the flat rock against the arrow notch, sending the arrow head punching through the young cowpoke's chest just below the collarbone.

Hamm gasped in surprise, then grimaced, muttered a string of curses, and passed out. Without any wasted movements, Mike snapped the metal head from the arrow, and in a quick jerk, extracted the arrow.

He pushed Hamm onto his stomach while he cleansed the ugly black hole and dumped a yellow powder in it. Turning the unconscious young man over, he did the same with the exit wound, then packed the bleeding holes with spider webs.

"He rest tonight. Ride tomorrow."

Next morning, Hamm Simmons gobbled down cold cornbread and sipped hot coffee. "It's sore," he said when Mary asked how he felt. "But there's no bad pain, and there ain't no bleeding." He glanced uncomfortably at Mike Gray-Eyes who was staring impassively into the small fire. Hamm cleared his throat. His voice was tentative when he said, "I'm much obliged."

Mike looked up at Ham. His black eyes flickered, his only response.

Reverend Matthew Adams was visiting Sheriff Rabb when Josh rode in and brought the sheriff up-to-date. Rabb shifted around on his bunk next to the wall and grimaced. "I was afraid of that. Whoever's behind the rustling is slicker than calf slobber."

Josh nodded. "They might be slick, but Mike Gray-Eyes is a heap slicker. We would have stayed out there if Hamm hadn't got himself hurt. I don't cotton to the idea that herds just up and vanish. They go somewhere, but the rain washed out all sign. Still I got me an idea about how they manage to up and disappear."

Sheriff Rabb arched an eyebrow. "How's that?"

"Just a wild guess, but I noticed thick deposits of limestone cross the trace."

"Reckon I've seen them. What about them?" The sheriff replied.

"Well, if I rustled me some beeves and wanted to throw a posse off, every time I reached one of those deposits, I'd drift ten or fifteen head off the trace. They'll leave sign, but sign that only sharp eyes can pick up. Indian eyes, not white man's."

"You plan on going back out tomorrow?"

"Nope, first, I want to ride up to Fort McKavett to see if they've been buying any beeves. If they have, then we'll see who's been doing the selling."

Reverend Adams laughed. "I hope you plan on being back by Sunday, Deputy. I know a young woman who'll be mighty disappointed if a certain somebody isn't there to buy her box with the yellow ribbon."

Josh glanced sheepishly at the sheriff. "So she told you about the yellow ribbon too, huh?"

The reverend laughed once again. "I think she's probably told everybody in town."

Ten minutes later as the reverend headed back to his parsonage beside the church, he met Sonora Fats riding down the street. The two locked eyes, then quickly looked away. The preacher had mixed feelings. His brother swore adamantly he was not one of the rustlers, and Matt Adams wanted to believe him. Still, it's hard to break a dog from egg-sucking. Maybe he should tell Elmer about the deputy's plan to visit Fort McKavett.

Mid-afternoon the next day, Sonora Fats peered out the dingy window of McCool's Saloon, watching curiously as Josh lashed his gear to the cantle of his saddle while Mike Gray-Eyes looked on from the back of his pinto.

"There he is," Grat Plummer muttered to Sonora Fats.

With a grunt, Fats motioned to one of his boys, Jim Selman, a gunnie from Arizona, whose specialty was bushwhacking unsuspecting victims.

Dressed in his trademark black, Selman sauntered lazily over to the window, his thumbs hooked in his gunbelt. "Yeah?"

Fats sucked on a tooth. "There he is. The Injun too if

you got a mind. Unlimber that Maypole, or whatever that fancy rifle of yours is and take care of him. From what I hear, he's heading up to Fort McKavett asking questions. Questions that I just as soon don't want to be asked."

Selman grunted. "It's a Maynard, a fifty-eight." He glanced up at his boss with cold eyes that hid his contempt for the fat man.

"Just make sure you're out of Kimble County, you hear?"

The killer grinned crookedly up at Sonora Fats. "You worry too much, Boss."

Grat Plummer arched an eyebrow. "How'd you find out they was heading up to Fort McKavett?"

Sonora Fats sneered. "Ain't none of your business," then he spit on the floor.

Josh and Mike Gray-Eyes spent the night at the Simmons' spread, riding out early next morning after the young deputy gently declined Mary Simmons' offer to ride along with them.

She protested. "But Hamm's fine. The medicine Mike Gray-Eyes gave him is working miracles. Pa and Kelt can look after Ed and Hamm."

Mike Gray-Eyes shot Josh a hard look. Josh knew exactly what the old Kickapoo was thinking, 'woman are trouble.'

Mary stood in the shade of the porch watching Josh and Mike Gray-Eyes ride out. She couldn't understand why he had refused her offer to ride along. She was as capable as any man in the county. She shook her head in disgust. Well, if he was going to be that stubborn, then he deserved whatever he got.

Josh and the old Indian disappeared around a bend in the road a half-a-mile distant. She turned to go back inside, but movement caught her eyes. She hesitated, peering down the road as a slender jasper dressed all in black emerged from the scrub live oak and trotted up the trail after Josh and Mike Gray-Eyes.

Tossing her blond hair from her eyes, Mary studied the rider. A tingly feeling sent shivers racing up her arms, and deep inside, there stirred the ominous intuition that the stranger was following Josh.

She rushed into the house and hastily changed into riding gear.

Chapter Twelve

The morning was clear, the air clean with just the slightest hint of winter on its edge. The morning grew warmer, and just before noon, Josh spotted Devil's Butte. He slowed his buckskin, his eyes quartering the tableland from the rocky slopes of the mesa to the thick shoreline of cattails along Viejo Creek.

Mike Gray-Eyes chuckled. "No Comanche around."

Josh shot him a glance. "You're sure?"

The old Kickapoo looked at Josh with disdain.

"All right, all right. Does that mean we can pull up at the creek yonder and boil some coffee?" He glanced at the sun directly overhead. "Taste good about now along with some of the biscuits Miss Mary packed."

Mike Gray-Eyes grunted.

Jim Selman was an accomplished assassin, well versed in the shadowy subterfuge of the hunter tracking the prey. He rode a hundred yards or so off the road, staying back in the mesquite and rolling hills, keeping Josh and the Indian in sight until the precise moment presented itself.

And that moment was rapidly approaching.

The task he was on now was a familiar one, one he had often undertaken with a success that had put his skills in great demand among those ambitious and eager to attain their own purposes by any means.

A cruel smile twisted his lips as he glanced down at the polished stock of his Maynard rifle, a .58 single shot that reached out over a thousand yards with deadly accuracy, an accuracy made even more certain by the powerful Davidson scope bolted to the receiver. His fingers caressed the weapon.

The hair on the back of Mary Simmons' neck stood on end as she followed the man in black who deliberately remained well off the narrow road that wound through the mesquite and liveoak tableland. That he was following Josh and Mike Gray-Eyes was obvious, but why? She was reluctant to draw close enough to discern the man's identity, content instead to remain far enough behind to blend in with the dusty mesquite and low hanging limbs of the liveoak.

Abruptly, she reined up and peered through the thick tangle of limbs and branches.

The man in black had halted. From where she sat on her bay, she could glimpse a portion of his torso and his horse's body, the position of which told her both man and horse were facing away from her. She looked beyond, spotting the purple ramparts of Devil's Butte silhouetted against the clear sky.

As she peered through the tangle of limbs, the rider's horse turned to the left. Mary remained motionless, watching the black figure drift through the mesquite. A frown knit her forehead. Now what was he up to? Or had she been mistaken that he was following Josh and the old Kickapoo?

She started to urge her bay forward, but hesitated, fearful her pony might give her away. Quickly, she dismounted and tied the bay to a mesquite. Shucking her Henry from the boot, she followed on foot.

Darting from tree to tree, the slight woman kept the rider in sight, freezing whenever he glanced over his shoulder. After a quarter of a mile, she began to question the wisdom of following on foot. If he were following Josh and Mike Gray-Eyes, why was he angling away from their trail?

And then she smelled the woodsmoke.

In that instant, not only did she know why he was moving at a sharp angle to their trail, but her intuition instantly presumed the reason behind it.

The woodsmoke had to be from Josh and Mike Gray-Eyes' noon camp, and whatever the man in black was up to, it was no good. Otherwise, why would he be skulking around like a weasel?

Then he turned his horse up the slope of the butte.

She hurried after him, crouching behind the trunk of an ancient liveoak at the base of the slope and peering over a thick limb as the wiry jasper leaned forward over his pony's neck while the short-coupled gray jitter-stepped up the steep slope.

Once, he paused and looked back, a frown on his face as he carefully scanned the slope beneath him. Mary pulled back behind the trunk of the liveoak, and whispered a short prayer.

She removed her hat and peered over the limb just in time to see him vanish over the rim. Quickly, she scurried up the steep grade after him, her feet slipping on the graveled slope.

Dropping to her stomach just below the rim, she snapped off her hat and peered over the lip of the mesa. The man in black had reined up several feet back from the far rim some three hundred feet distant. He dismounted and extracted a scoped rifle from a boot beneath the saddle fender. He broke it open at the breech and inserted a brass cartridge.

Mary stared in disbelief. Her breath caught in her throat. The hombre she had been following was planning on ambushing Josh and Mike Gray-Eyes. Her heart pounded like a blacksmith's hammer.

Jim Selman ran his hands lovingly over the cold metal of the Maynard rifle. This finely built rifle was the one certainty in his life; the one invariable that never failed him; the one constant that never let him down.

Gently, he removed the caps from the four-power Davidson scope, then lowered himself to his knees and crawled to the edge of the rim where he dropped to his belly. With the nip in the late October air, the warm sun on his back felt good. Winter was knocking on the door, he told himself, just like I'm about to knock on the deputy and the Indian's door.

Easing the muzzle of the Maynard over the rim, he settled the butt into his shoulder and shifted his body until his eye was peering comfortably into the eyepiece of the scope.

Down below, the small fire came into focus. He adjusted his position to the scope and picked up the back of Josh's head. Moving the muzzle ever so slightly, he lined up the crosshairs on Mike Gray-Eyes forehead. He touched the tip of his finger to the trigger, then pulled it away.

"The deputy first," he muttered. "Then the cripple."

Mary Simmons stared in disbelief. Her brain screamed to shoot at the prone man, but her muscles refused to move.

"Move, you silly woman, move," she muttered, but her fingers remained frozen around the pistol grip of the Henry stock.

Selman shifted his lean body inches to the left and peered into the scope, centering the cross hairs on the hatband around the Stetson the deputy wore. At that point, the slug would rip through the back of the brain and exit the chin, taking with it the entire lower half of the deputy's face. He touched his finger to the trigger gently, tightened the pressure, drew a deep breath, and held it.

Suddenly a stunning thud exploded in his ears and ripped the Maynard from his hands. The impact rolled

him over onto his back. Another crack, and a chunk of
dirt exploded several feet from him. He rolled over
again, this time tumbling over the edge of the rim and
sliding down the steep slope. He slammed into a boulder, dazing him momentarily.

Shouts jerked him from his stupor. He staggered to
his feet, shucking his six-gun. From below, he heard
startled voices.

Above, a shrill voice shouted, "He's got a gun, Josh."

With a curse, Selman spun and fired. The slug tore a
chunk out of the rim at Mary's feet. She threw herself
backward and, regaining her feet, bolted for the far side
of the butte.

Selman started up the slope, but a shout from below
froze him in his tracks. He spun as Josh skirted a boulder and raced up the trail, disappearing behind a jagged
upthrust of yellow limestone.

His eyes narrowing in bloodlust, the hired killer
slipped into a fissure overlooking the trail and lined up
the muzzle of his .44 Remington revolver on the limestone outcropping from behind which he expected Josh
to emerge at any moment. A cruel grin stretched his
thin lips over bared teeth as he tightened his finger on
the trigger, ready to touch it off.

Suddenly, the deputy materialized on the opposite
side of the outcropping, tossing off two quick shots from
his Henry before darting back behind the limestone.

The lead slugs splatted into the side of the fissure
wall in front of Jim Selman, ricocheted off the opposite

wall, then back again, the shards of lead and limestone stinging the hired killer's face.

Cursing between clenched teeth, he jumped forward, fired three times at the outcroppings, then leaped back into the fissure.

No sooner had he fallen back into the crevice, two more shots ripped the air from below, slamming into the fissure and ricocheting off the limestone walls. One of the smashed slugs tore into the inside of Selman's thigh.

A scream ripped from the killer's lips. He grabbed at the inside of his thigh and felt hot blood coursing through his fingers. He looked down, staring in disbelief at the great jets of bright red blood gushing between his fingers, turning the yellow limestone black and giving a shiny sheen to his black trousers.

A great roaring filled his ears as a wave of fury swept over the gunman. This was not supposed to happen to him. It was always someone else, not him. With a scream of rage and a string of curses, he leaped from the fissure and fired at the limestone outcropping.

So blinded by the frenzy of his anger, he never felt the two hundred and twenty grain slugs slam into his chest. He never felt his body slam to the ground. Jim Selman did not even feel his life draining from him. All his numbed brain could process was that the blue sky above was quickly turning dark.

Chapter Thirteen

His finger on the trigger, Josh paused at Selman's body. The glaze across the owlhoot's open eyes was mute testimony the bushwhacker was dead. Holstering his six-gun, he hurried on up the slope. Mike Gray-Eyes' shout stopped him just short of the rim. "Watch out. Woman might shoot you."

Josh jerked to a halt. He looked back down the slope. The old Kickapoo was shaking his head, a rueful grin on his ancient lips. Josh raised an eyebrow. The old Indian might be right. He cupped his hand to his lips. "Hold off, Mary. It's me, Josh." Then he stuck his head tentatively over the rim of the mesa.

A hundred yards away, a head popped up from below the other rim. "That you, Josh? Are you all right?"

Josh had to grin. He would have given a thousand to

one odds that would have been her first question. "Thanks to you," he shouted back. "How about you?"

"Fine."

After retrieving her pony, Mary related the events of the morning around the small campfire. "I never got close enough to recognize him, but I knew something was wrong when he stayed off the trail like he did. And then when he pulled out that rifle—" She paused, looking around at the smashed rifle beside the fire. "I've never seen one like that with that tube on top."

"It's a scope. Magnifies things far away." Josh nodded to the body draped over the saddle. "Now that you've had a closer look at this jasper, do you know who he is?"

"No. I've seen him around town, usually coming out or going into the saloon."

Mike Gray-Eyes and Josh exchanged knowing looks. The deputy rose to his feet and kicked dirt over the fire. "Well, I reckon we get this hombre back to town and see if anyone can give him a name. We'll drop you off at your place on the way, Miss Mary."

At the Simmons' spread, Josh declined an invitation to supper. "Obliged, but we best get this old boy back to town before he ripens. Find out who he is. And if we're lucky," he added. "Maybe find out who sent him."

Mary hid her disappointment. With a hopeful gleam in her eye, she said, "You still plan to go to the box dinner Sunday at church, don't you?"

He nodded. "I know. A yellow ribbon."

The young woman beamed, and to his own surprise, Josh found himself looking forward to the box dinner.

The sun was dropping behind the rugged hills to the west as they rode into Junction Flats. Josh pulled up to the hitching rail, but Mike Gray-Eyes continued south. The deputy said nothing, knowing the old Indian's penchant for avoiding any confrontation with the white man. "I'll be out to the shack later."

Sheriff Rabb hobbled out to the horse at the rail. Leaning on his crutch, he grabbed the dead man's long hair and pulled his head up. "Yep, seen him around. Think his name is Selman. Runs with that owlhoot Sonora Fats along with half-a-dozen other no-goods. Why don't you go over to the saloon and get McCool. He'll know for sure. Fats is always hanging out over there."

Slick McCool studied the face in the light of the lantern Josh held. He straightened his shoulders and pulled out a thin cheroot and touched a match to it. He blew out a stream of smoke and nodded. "Yep. Jim Selman. That's who it is. Looks better now than I've seen him in quite a spell."

Sheriff Rabb grunted. "Runs with Sonora Fats, ain't that right?"

McCool arched an eyebrow. "Runs? I don't know about that, but sometimes when I see Fats, Selman is around." He paused, a faint grin curling his lips. "I mean, was."

"You seen them the last couple days?"

After pondering the question a moment, the dapper saloon owner nodded. "Yesterday. Around noon or some thereafter, if I remember right."

Josh glanced at the sheriff who nodded slowly. "Thanks, McCool. Appreciate your help."

With an amiable grin, the saloon owner touched a thin finger to his forehead. "Always glad to lend a hand to the local law, Sheriff."

Josh and Rabb watched as McCool strolled back to the saloon. "Sounds to me like this Selman jasper followed me out of town."

"It do sound like that, don't it?"

"You think McCool knew I was riding up to Fort McKavett?"

The sheriff studied the retreating back of Slick McCool. "How could he know that? I didn't tell anyone. The only other one who knew was the preacher, and he wouldn't say nothing."

"What about this Sonora Fats. Is he wanted for anything?"

Sheriff Rabb turned around awkwardly with his crutch. He drew a deep breath and paused before he tried to step up on the boardwalk. "Not around here. I've wondered about him. From what I hear, he's got a shirt-tail outfit back west, out past old Fort Terrett. But, far as I know, he's clean in the other counties. Of course," he added, giving Josh a wry look. "Like I told you before, I sometimes wonder about the law in them other counties."

Josh gave the sheriff a helping hand up onto the boardwalk. "I'll take Selman on down to the undertaker, and then between you and me, I'll ride back out tonight. I can reach the butte before midnight, catch a nap, then hit the fort by mid-morning."

Slick McCool paused on the porch in front of his saloon to watch Josh lead Selman's pony down to the undertaker. He shook his head. Apparently, Jim Selman's bold talk couldn't match the deputy's six-gun.

Raucous laughter erupted from inside. Sonora Fats! A crooked grin slid over McCool's angular face. He hooked his thumbs in the pockets of his silk vest. He couldn't wait to see the face of the fat man when he heard about Selman's fate.

Sonora Fats glared at McCool in disbelief, the sweat on the fat man's face glistening in the yellow light cast by the overhead lanterns. "Selman? You right certain, McCool? It was Selman? Nobody guns down Jim Selman."

Behind Fats, Grat Plummer and Rowdy Joe Lowe gaped up at the saloon owner.

"Well, if it isn't Selman, it's his twin. The deputy just hauled him down to the undertaker draped over the saddle of that big gray he rode."

Slamming his glass of whiskey down on the table at his side, Sonora Fats brushed past the grinning saloon owner. "I don't believe you," he growled. "The only way anyone could get to him is in the back when he wasn't looking."

McCool chuckled and ambled back to his table in the rear of the saloon.

While Josh camped at Devil's Butte that night, Sonora Fats sat in McCool's Saloon, getting drunker by the minute. "Nobody," he muttered, slurring his words. "Nobody kills a friend of mine and gets away with it." He glared at Grat and Rowdy through bleary, bloodshot eyes. "You hear what I say? Huh?"

Grat Plummer cast a sidelong glance at Slick McCool seated at a rear table, sipping on whiskey and idly watching his customers mix and mingle. "Don't talk so loud, Fats. Somebody might hear you."

The fat man grunted. He cut his black eyes toward McCool. Grat was right. Best he keep his intentions to himself. He pushed to his feet and staggered from the saloon. Grat Plummer and Rowdy Lowe tagged after him.

Josh rode into Fort McKavett at mid-morning. A tinge of guilt washed over him when he spotted the young soldiers wearing butternut uniforms. He tried to push it aside. He reminded himself he had spent almost three years doing his duty, a voluntary enlistment longer than most Southerners served, and unlike many, he had not paid one cent for a slave to take his place. Still, he could not shake the guilt nagging at his conscience.

The Procurement Officer, Lieutenant John Keith, was due in from patrol later in the day, but not a single enlisted man in the Quartermaster's Office would provide Josh the information he sought. "Canna help, Deputy," replied a young corporal in a thick Irish brogue. "The lieutenant, he'd be taking a shillelah upside my bleedin' head. T'is sorry I am."

Josh thanked the young man and led his buckskin over to the local livery where he unsaddled the pony and grained him. "Take it easy for a few hours, Buck," he said, running his fingers through the buckskin's black mane in an effort to work out some tangles.

The horse looked around. He fluttered his black lips, but Josh cautioned. "Watch it. You know what happened last time you tried to bite me."

Buck eyed him a moment, then turned back to his grain.

Josh's stomach growled though he had cinched his belt up to the last notch. He chuckled to his pony. "Either I got to punch me another hole or find me some grub to put myself around."

He ambled next door to the saloon where he felt more at ease than at the post and where a dime bought him a cool beer and a turn at the buffet table of cold cuts. He built a sandwich of thick sliced hog ham and sharp cheese slathered over with mustard. With a dill pickle to top off his repast, he slid into a chair at one of the vacant tables.

The saloon did a steady business. In the hour or so he

sat at the table, a couple dozen cowpokes wandered in, downed a beer or two, then moseyed out.

One, an amiable looking jasper in run over boots and threadbare duds built a sandwich Josh swore the young puncher would have to dislocate his jaw to get his lips around. When the grinning cowboy spotted Josh watching him, he sauntered over, and with a friendly smile, said, "Mind if I join you, Stranger. I just rode in, and I hate to eat alone. I'll even buy you another beer," he added, seeing the empty mug in front of Josh.

Josh nodded to the chair. "Glad for the company. I'll take care of the beer."

The young stranger was a drifter from up Colorado way. Ben Caruthers from Denver. "Yep, had no place to go, and truth is, I was mighty tired of all the cold. Heard South Texas was warm enough to sweat down a tallow candle. That was for me. Why, even a job offer up near Topeka to help survey railroad right-of-ways down to San Antone couldn't change my mind. Now, if it was starting down in San Antone and surveying up, I might have considered the notion. But like I said, I been hankering for warm weather."

Josh had relaxed, his mind drifting, but the mention of a railroad jerked him back to the present. "What's that you say? A railroad? To San Antone?"

Young Ben gobbled a mouthful of sandwich. "Yes, sir. The T.T.&S. has surveyed all the way down to Texas. Right now, they're doing their blasted best to survey and buy up property from the Texas border on down to San Antone."

Suddenly, a few pieces of a puzzle of which Josh had not even been aware jumped into his head. The railroad! And land!

Who was it, old Joe Windham who had sold out only a few months back for pennies on the dollar? And now, Hank Bartholomew was facing the same fate.

And, according to Archer Simmons, the Circle S wasn't far behind.

And strangely enough, all three ranches were north of Junction Flats, together covering about twenty or thirty miles north to south, a nice chunk of right-of-way for someone interested in making a sale to the railroad. Could it be, he asked himself, that the rustling was part of the effort to buy up the land at dirt-cheap prices?

Josh tried to ply more information from the young puncher, but Ben Caruthers knew nothing more.

About that time, the young corporal from the Quartermaster's Office hurried in, paused inside the door, scanned the room, then came directly to Josh.

"The lieutenant just rode in, Mr. Barkley. He be waiting for you."

As soon as Josh pushed through the batwing doors of the saloon and spotted the post, the sense of guilt came flooding back. Let's get this over with in a hurry, he told himself.

Lieutenant John Keith was typical career cavalry out

of West Point and determined to finish the war as a captain. He sat stiffly behind his desk and gestured to a straight back chair in front of the desk. "So, how may I be of service to you, Mr. Barkley?"

Josh quickly explained the purpose of his mission.

The lieutenant briskly replied. "We have indeed purchased two or three herds from down around Mason and Gillespie Counties in the last two years." He nodded emphatically. "Good stock. Good beeves, but they're not the ones you're looking for. These all had a legitimate bill of sale. I just hope the supplier can keep providing them for us."

Josh nodded. "Can you tell me who signed the bill of sale?"

The lieutenant eyed him suspiciously.

Josh explained. "Like I said, Lieutenant. There's been some rustling going on. I just want to make sure you're getting legitimate stock."

Lieutenant Keith considered Josh's explanation. He nodded briefly. "Certainly." He strode to his desk, opened a drawer, and thumbed through a file. "Let's see," he muttered. "Here it is." He read the name once or twice as if to commit it to memory. "The man who signed the last three bill of sales was from Junction Flats."

Josh nodded. "And the name?"

The lieutenant looked up at Josh. "William McCool."

Chapter Fourteen

McCool! William 'Slick' McCool!

And the nickname was most fitting, Josh told himself.

With an arch of an eyebrow, the lieutenant said, "You must know McCool if you're from Junction Flats, Deputy."

Josh nodded. "I know him. He's well respected." He lied. "I'm just surprised he took time to bring the herd in. He usually stays close to Junction Flats."

The lieutenant shook his head. "You misunderstand. McCool didn't bring them in. I've never met the gentleman. His ramrod was the one who I dealt with, a jasper dressed all in black." He frowned. "His name escapes me, but—"

All in black! Josh stiffened, then forced himself to relax. "You probably mean Jim Selman."

"That's it. Selman."

120

"Good man." Josh lied once again. "Tell me, Lieutenant. The beeves you bought, you have a record of the brands?"

Lieutenant Keith thumbed through the sheath of papers in his hand. "Certainly. There were several, all legitimately signed over to Mr. McCool."

"Do you mind if I take a look." Josh extended his hand. "Not at all."

Josh scanned the brands, noting the Rising Sun, the Pick and Shovel, the Flying W, and, the Circle B. He handed them back. "I didn't see any Circle S stock," he commented, thinking of the Simmons' spread and the rustled herd.

Keith shrugged. "If isn't on the list, we haven't purchased any."

"I see." Josh rose from his chair and extended his hand. "Well, thanks for the information, Lieutenant."

With a single shake of his head, Lieutenant Keith replied. "Sorry I couldn't be of any more help, Deputy."

Josh grinned. "No, you were more help than you know, Lieutenant."

"Good." He glanced out the window. "It's getting late. You're welcome to spend the night. We always have extra bunks down in the doghouse."

"Much obliged, but I'm running short on grub. I need to pick up some at the commissary and then try to make a few miles before dark."

The lieutenant grinned ruefully. "About all we got at the commissary until the supply train comes in is Mr. Lincoln's shingles."

Josh chuckled. "Lordy, Lieutenant, I grew up on hard bread and blackstrap syrup."

Five minutes later, Josh rode out, relieved to leave the fort and his guilty conscience behind. He glanced over his shoulder and spotted dark clouds rolling in from the north. He muttered a soft curse. Once those clouds reached him, it would be so dark he couldn't find his nose with both hands.

He rode hard over the winding road of limestone cobbles, his mind trying to fit together just what was happening back in Mason and Gillespie Counties. What he had learned from the lieutenant didn't make sense. Why would McCool sign his own name to the bills of sale if the cattle had been rustled unless he was in on it?

After all, Selman was one of Sonora Fats' hardcases before Josh sent the gunman tripping down the staircase to Hades. And Fats was chummy with McCool. He hung out in the saloon, and on more than one occasion, Josh had personally seen the two in deep conversation.

If there was any connection between the two, McCool had to be the brains. Mental brainpower did not appear to be an overpowering strength of Sonora Fats and his hardcases.

Of course, he told himself. Their partnership could be the obvious reason Fats kept his nose clean in Junction Flats and Kimble County. The rustlers needed a refuge, and thanks to Slick McCool, they had one in Junction Flats.

A frown knit his forehead as another question puzzled him. If McCool was behind the rustling, where was the Simmons' herd? Sheriff Rabb claimed Sonora Fats was running a shirt-tailed outfit around old Fort Terrett. Could he have moved the herd out there?

Thirty minutes after sundown, the wind in his face began to swirl. Josh glanced over his back and grimaced. Dark clouds rolled across the treetops, bearing down on him. He leaned forward and patted Buck on the neck. "Well, Boy, I reckon we best find us a place to hole up for the night."

Ahead, he spotted a dry creek bed that disappeared around a small, but rugged hill. On the far side of the hill, he discovered a small cave cut into the limestone several feet above the creek bed. By stretching a canvas fly between the limestone overhang and two of the scrub oaks in front of the cave, he and Buck would be out of the weather for the most part. A small fire in the rear of the cave would provide heat. A tangle of dried branches and limbs filled a corner of the creek bed across from the cave, deposited there by earlier flash floods.

The clouds moved in as Josh quickly strung up the fly. By the time he had a small fire blazing, the rain had begun to fall and the temperature to plummet.

Josh had a sinking feeling that he was staring into the icy teeth of an early blue norther, those deadly storms that come out of nowhere and dump ice and snow five or ten inches deep. Quickly, he gathered more wood from the tangle of driftwood across the dry creek bed.

While water dripped from the fly above and ran down the back of the cave, Josh remained warm and fairly dry in his tarp-wrapped soogan. Hot coffee and Lincoln's shingles made as satisfying a repast as he could have hoped under the conditions outside. Some blackstrap syrup would have been right tasty, but the post commissary's supply had been depleted. Josh had to content himself dunking the hard bread in his coffee to soften it.

Back to the north, a dull roar broke the steady pounding of the rain. The roar grew louder, and the trickle of water running down the creek bed began to swell. The roaring intensified, and without warning, a three-foot wall of water swept around the hill, carrying with it broken limbs and small trees.

Josh watched the rising water warily as the level inched closer and closer to his camp. The water continued to rise until around midnight when the rain turned to snow. Soon the level of the creek began to fall. Josh relaxed. He fed a few more branches to the fire, then lay back on his saddle and pulled his blankets about his neck. He looked up at Buck, who, head down, eyes closed, gave every indication of sleeping. "Might as well join you, boy. We can't do nothing about anything right now."

And then he pulled the tarp over his head.

Throughout the night, tiny flakes of snow whipped under the fly, settling on the tarp. When Josh awakened the next morning, the snow was still drifting down.

Overhead, the canvas fly sagged from the weight of the fallen snow.

He climbed to his feet, stomped the circulation back into his legs, and built up the banked fire. Within minutes, his coffee was boiling and he had saddled Buck. "Don't figure the storm will last much longer. Best we move on." He stared thoughtfully into the falling snow. "Maybe," he muttered. "I might swing by Sonora Fats' spread and see what I can see."

Reverend Matthrew Adams looked up from his breakfast of corn mush and syrup at the knock on the door. Before he could reply, the door opened and Lester Boles scurried inside, his collar turned up, his hat pulled down over his ears against the weather, and a heavy woolen muffler wrapped around his neck. A coating of snow lay on his shoulders.

"Now what, Lester?" The reverend asked impatiently.

The diminutive postmaster ignored the sarcasm in the preacher's words. "Just heard. For certain this time. The supply train with sixty-thousand in gold is due in next Sunday. They plan to spend the night in Junction Flats, then head on down to Kerrville." He paused, his small, black eyes glittering with excitement. "This is what we've been waiting for. All the other times, the pickings were slim as a bedslat. This time, we can strike a damaging blow for the Union, one that could break the back of the Johnny Rebs in Texas."

The announcement sent a surge of excitement

through Matt Adams not because of the war effort, but because of the fifteen thousand dollar payment for information setting up the theft.

He pushed back from the table. "I'll leave right away. I can reach Rohmann by noon. He can contact the others by nightfall."

Boles nodded enthusiastically. "You think they'll hit the gold before or after Junction Flats?"

The preacher studied the animated face of the post-master with disdain. The little man truly believed in his mission. He was the kind of idealist who would die for a cause.

Adams sneered inwardly. What a fool, an idealistic fool who would have undertaken the task even if the money had not been offered. Money was all that was important, and with his share of the fifteen thousand plus what he had on deposit in St. Louis, by this time next year, he'd be living the good life down in South America—away from his past and away from his brother.

Reverend Adams cleared his throat. "We don't need to know where they plan on hitting the supply train. Our job is to pass along information when the gold is due. That's all." He reached for his greatcoat. "Now, best you get back to the post office. I've a long ride ahead of me."

When the storm failed to abate, Josh put off swinging by Fort Terrett, instead, he cut directly across the tableland of mesquite and liveoak toward Junction

Flats, bypassing the Simmons' spread on the east. The snow continued to fall, hindering his vision to around a quarter mile.

Through the tangle of mesquite and oak limbs, he spotted Viejo Creek. An unbroken mantle of snow covered the cattails lining the banks of the creek. Suddenly, Josh reined up. A horse and rider emerged from the thick snow on the east side of the creek and cut north along the Viejo. He stifled his first impulse to call out, suddenly curious as to why anyone would be out in such a storm. He backed Buck behind an ancient mesquite, hoping his outline would be blurred and distorted by the skeleton-like branches of the tree.

The rider grew even with Josh and continued north. To the deputy's surprise, he recognized the horseman as Reverend Matthew Adams. He frowned. What in the Sam Hill was Adams doing up here?

Buck stutter-stepped nervously. "Easy, Buck, easy." Josh laid a gentling hand on the buckskin's neck, feeling the tenseness of the animal's muscles.

After Adams disappeared into the snowfall, Josh headed upstream, following the preacher, but remaining on his side of the creek and far back in the mesquite.

Ten minutes later, Josh spotted an old shack beneath the snow-laden limbs of a spreading live oak. "Whoa, Buck, whoa." Smoke curled out of the stovepipe chimney and was quickly lost in the falling snow. Moments later, Adams reappeared and headed down his backtrail.

Josh wasn't a churchgoing hombre, but he'd seen

enough ceremonies and rituals to know that none of them were as brief as was Adams' visit. Even a shotgun marriage with a lick, a promise, and a thank you ma'am lasted longer that the preacher's stay inside the shack.

And to the deputy's surprise, moments after Adams rode away, a thin man hurried out to his rawhide and pole barn. Two minutes later, he headed east in a gallop, his pony throwing up rooster tails of snow from its hooves.

Josh frowned. Why east? He shook his head. In the last half hour since he spotted Reverend Adams, events had taken a suspicious turn. No soul ventured out on a day like this unless it was a matter of life or death.

Only one thought came to his mind. Could the two be part of the rustling? He shook his head. No. Maybe whoever the jasper who lived in the shack, but not the preacher. But then, what was the preacher doing here?

He studied the two riders as they drew apart. On impulse, Josh followed the slender man.

By mid-afternoon, a solid eight inches of snow covered the ground, drifting to several feet in arroyos and gullies and on the windward side of boulders.

As the storm intensified, Josh drew closer to the small cowpoke so as not to lose sight of him. Finally, the slender man reined up at the base of a slope leading up between two sheer walls of limestone. He twisted around in his saddle, deliberately searching the tableland behind him. Josh pulled up behind some scrub oak and watched.

After a moment, the cowpoke spurred his pony and rode into the canyon.

Josh hung back, scanning the canyon rims for any sentries. Dark fissures in the snow-covered walls of sheer limestone stared back at him, fissures that could hold one or a dozen sentries.

Suddenly, a cold voice sounded from behind him. "Get your eyes full, Johnny Reb. You ain't going to see no more."

Josh froze. His brain raced. "Hold on, Mister. I'm just passing through. I don't know what you're talking about." He glanced over his shoulder and spotted a bearded cowpoke standing on the ground behind him, holding a breech loading Sharps aimed at the middle of Josh's back. He wore a dark blue greatcoat and a woolen scarf tied over his hat and knotted under his chin.

The bearded jasper snorted. "Ain't nobody passing through in this here kind of weather."

Tossing his head, Buck looked around at the voice.

Josh pressed his right leg into Buck's ribs, forcing the buckskin to move to his left. "I ain't saying I'm real bright, Mister, but the gospel truth is that was just what I was doing. A short piece back, I spotted that hombre that just went up that canyon and was following him, figuring he might take me to a town where I can put myself around some hot grub and find a warm bed."

"Well, they ain't no town around here, and you ain't going to need no warm bed."

Josh felt Buck's muscles tense. Suddenly the buckskin threw his haunches up and lashed out with his hooves. The bearded cowpoke screamed. The Sharps discharged, and Josh wheeled about and raced for the protection of the liveoak and mesquite.

As Buck dashed through the snow, gunshots broke the silence of the cold morning. Josh leaned forward over the straining horse's neck.

Suddenly, a numbing blow hit him on the side of the head. He felt himself slipping into the black depths of unconsciousness. Desperately, he tangled his fingers in the buckskin's black mane, hoping to hold on. Time blurred, and then he felt himself falling and falling into a dark pit that grew ever deeper and darker by the moment.

Chapter Fifteen

Voices awakened Josh. Overhead, stars glittered against the cold blackness of the icy heavens. Every muscle in his body shivered, trying to fight off the chilling cold. He lay without moving, staring up at the stars through a tunnel of snow down through which voices drifted.

"We done looked far enough. That jasper's gone."

Josh recognized the voice as belonging to the hombre who had pulled down on him back at the canyon.

"You reckon he was what he said, just a drifter? We come too far to lose out now."

"Yep. He was a drifter. You could tell by looking. Just a no-account saddle tramp. Let's get on back."

"What about his horse? We can follow his tracks."

"You find the critter if you want to. Me, I'm heading

back. I'm freezing my boot heels off. If that jasper is out here somewhere, he won't last the night."

The voices faded away.

Josh grimaced, suddenly conscious of a dull ache throbbing on the side of his head. He closed his eyes against the pain and tried to remember how he had come to be lying here in the snow. All he could recollect was racing from the canyon and then a numbing blow struck him.

He tried to roll over, but a something sharp jabbed his side. He grimaced, and the throbbing in his head intensified. He rolled back to his left, and suddenly there came a sharp crack, and the bed of snow on which he lay fell out from under him, sending him tumbling down through a tangle of snapping branches until he slammed into the ground.

His head exploded. A strangled groan escaped between his clenched teeth. He lay motionless, waiting for the searing pain to subside, for his breath to come back.

As the pain eased, he opened his eyes. All he could see was the stars above. Gingerly, he extended his hand into the darkness surrounding him. He jerked back when a sharp branch jabbed the palm of his hand.

A few seconds more of probing the darkness, and Josh realized he was lying beneath a large bush or even a small tree, a willow, he guessed from the limber branches he could feel.

Clenching his teeth against the pounding in his head, he rolled over on his hands and knees and managed to stand, pushing aside limbs depressed by the weight of the snow. He felt his arms and legs gingerly. Other than a head pounding like a hangover from a week-long drunk, nothing seemed busted or broke.

His first step was to dig himself out of the snowdrift. He shoved his arm into the snow and felt it break through. A grin played over his lips. Only a foot or so.

Brief minutes later, he broke through the drift and clambered to the rim of the arroyo into which he had tumbled when he fell from his buckskin.

The starlight reflected off the snow, providing sufficient illumination for Josh to follow the tracks of his horse. His head continued to throb, but the exertion of lumbering through the snow warmed him, driving away the chills racking his body only minutes earlier.

Soon the sun rose, a great, blood-red ball that for a few moments turned the horizon black as a raven's wing. Within minutes, the red burned off, and as far as the eye could see, the morning sun glistened off the new fallen snow like millions of fresh-cut diamonds, forcing Josh to squint into the glare.

Just before noon, he spotted Buck back among some boulders on the side of a mesa, probably grazing on dry grass protected from the snow, he guessed. The buckskin whinnied when he spotted Josh and promptly trotted a few steps away from his owner.

"Easy, boy," Josh muttered. "Easy."

Buck trotted off a few more steps.

Josh cursed. "Blast you, Buck. Take it easy."

The buckskin eyed him warily, then shied away once again.

Biting his tongue, Josh eased toward the buckskin, and in a cajoling whisper, called out, "Hey, there, boy. Easy does it. Easy, easy."

Muscles trembling, ready to bolt, Buck stood staring at Josh, but for reasons known only to the animal, he remained motionless, allowing Josh to slide his fingers under the bridle.

Breathing a sigh of relief, Josh managed to climb into the saddle and point Buck for Junction Flats.

Josh winced as Doc Sears examined the knot on the side of his head. "Easy, Doc. That's sore as a carbuncle."

The old doctor snorted. "You best be glad you got a head on those shoulders to be sore, Deputy. Another half inch and the whole side of your head would be gone." He finished daubing the wound with carbolic acid. "There. I reckon if that acid can clean up my tools, it blasted well ought to burn away any infection. Reckon that's about all I can do." He stood upright and rolled his shoulders in an effort to stretch his back. "You say you never saw where the shot came from?"

"Nope."

Doc Sears looked around at the sheriff. "Those rustlers are either getting a heap braver or a lot more skittish."

Rabb arched an eyebrow. "I hope it's skittish."

Looking back at Josh, the doctor said, "You'd be smart to let me look at that head tomorrow." He shot

Sheriff Rabb a wry glance. "But, knowing you lawmen, you'll probably go out of your way not to take yourself."

The sheriff chuckled. "Now, Doc. You know better'n that. Why—"

Doc Sears waved him off. "Don't hand me no lies, August Rabb. I knowed you too long."

After the doctor left, the sheriff turned back to Josh. "All right. Now, what were you telling me about you getting potshot when the doc came in?"

Josh poured himself a cup of coffee and touched a match to his fresh-built cigarette. Squinting into the smoke, he said. "Well, the potshot was after Fort McKavett and after I spotted the local preacher, Reverend Adams."

The sheriff frowned. "The preacher? Fort McKavett?" he shook his head. "You best go back and cut the deck a little deeper on that, deputy."

Taking a deep breath, Josh grunted. "All right, first, the preacher. I was coming back from the fort when I spotted him just before I reached Viejo Creek. It was snowing something fierce. He was coming from the direction of town. When he reached the creek, he turned north. I followed him up to a squatter's shack."

The sheriff reached for the bag of Bull Durham. "Sounds like Lee Rohmann's place. You see him? Small man?"

"Yeah."

"Go on."

Quickly sketching out all which followed, Josh

added. "So, when Adams left the shack, I followed this Rohmann jasper. I was about to go in the canyon after him when some hombre pulled down on me from behind."

Sheriff Rabb struck a match on the side of his leg and touched it to the cigarette. "What then?"

Leaning forward, Josh continued. "He said something funny, Sheriff. Something that made me think he was involved in more than rustling."

"He said something? Like what?"

He said, "Get your eyes full, Johnny Reb. You ain't going to see no more."

Sheriff Rabb frowned. "Johnny Reb? So?"

"So, stop and consider it, Sheriff. Down here, we're all Southerners. Johnny Reb is a Yankee expression— short for *Johnny Rebel* because of this war the Yankees make out to be a rebellion."

For several moments, the sheriff pondered Josh's words. He replied thoughtfully. "Off and on, the talk of federal spies comes up hereabouts, but nothing's ever come of it. I figure it's just war talk. Could be, on the other hand, we might have us a band of rustlers working for the north."

Josh grimaced. "That doesn't wash. If that was so, then why would Union sympathizers sell the beeves to the south?"

"They wouldn't."

"But, the garrison at Fort McKavett is buying from the rustlers."

"How can you be certain?"

The setting sun filled the jail with a reddish glow as Josh poured another cup of coffee. "The procurement officer, Lieutenant Keith, has bought two or three small herds of beef from Mason and Gillespie Counties. The brands were the Rising Sun, the Pick and Shovel, the Flying W and the Circle B." He paused. "All from herds that have been hit by the rustlers."

Sheriff Rabb arched an eyebrow. "Maybe them ranchers sold those particular beeves to the army."

"They didn't, and I'll tell you why. Take a guess at who the jasper is that the army's been dealing on each herd." Before the sheriff could respond, Josh told him. "Jim Selman, the hombre I brought in a while back draped over his saddle."

"Selman!" The sheriff's eyes grew wide.

Josh added, "And that isn't all. The bill of sale had been signed each time by Slick McCool."

"McCool!"

"McCool. Not the ranchers, but McCool."

"Maybe the ranchers sold them to McCool."

Josh shrugged. "Maybe. I aim to find out." He paused, then continued. "And you know that McCool's been buying up land." He sipped his coffee and retrieved the bag of Bull Durham from his vest pocket.

"Well, reckon he's never made no bones about that. Word about town is he figures enough land makes a gent respectable."

Josh shrugged. "I don't know about that, but what makes this so interesting is the railroad has plans to run tracks from Kansas City to San Antone. What about the

Windham Ranch back north of Hank Bartholomew? I heard it sold a few months back."

Sheriff Rabb pursed his lips and nodded thoughtfully. "Yep. Reckon it did, and I reckon you can guess who bought it."

Josh arched an eyebrow. "McCool?"

The sheriff grunted. "McCool."

"If he buys up the Bartholomew and Simmons' spread, then he'll have almost thirty miles of railroad right-of-way. Could make a gent a mighty rich man, buy a heap of respectability."

The sheriff studied Josh for several moments. "Makes a man wonder, don't it?" He paused, noticing the frown that came over Josh's face. "What's wrong?"

"Truth is, with all this about McCool looking so guilty, something's puzzling me."

"Like what?"

"Why would McCool sign his own name to the bills of sale if he was behind the rustling?"

"Maybe he didn't reckon anyone would find out."

"Maybe."

Stubbing out his cigarette on the pot-bellied stove, the sheriff continued. "You know as well as me Selman was one of Sonora Fats' hardcases, and you know that Fats is right chummy with McCool. More than once, I've seen the two of them out on the porch in front of the saloon in what looked like a important conversation."

Josh's frown deepened. "That's what I mean, Sheriff. None of this fits together the way it should. It's too obvious. I can't figure McCool turned to rustling to get the money to buy out the ranches, figuring on getting rich after the war."

Sheriff Rabb sipped his coffee and arched an eyebrow. "How does he know who's going to win?"

Josh's eyebrow knit in pain. "That isn't hard to guess, Sheriff. Truth is, the war isn't going the way we want it. The North has too many factories for us. They're outproducing us. The South is running out of everything."

The sheriff studied Josh for several moments curiously. "For a drifter, you seem to know a right smart about what's going on out there." He twirled the tip of his mustache around one finger. "Was you in the war?"

Taking a long drag off his cigarette, Josh felt the guilt come flooding back. He studied the sheriff, the older man's craggy face, his ice-blue eyes.

Suddenly tired of carrying a guilty conscience everywhere he went, he replied, "For almost three years—up until last November. That's when my whole unit was destroyed in Georgia. When I woke up, everyone around me was dead. And I was about ready to roll into the grave." He drew a deep breath and stared at the sheriff defiantly. "That's when I knew we had lost even though the war wasn't over. I figured then I'd done my share." He paused, drew a deep breath, and added. "And so, for better or worse, here I am."

Sheriff Rabb studied the younger man thoughtfully. "Three years, you say?"

Josh nodded.

"A long time. Longer than most. You was lucky you didn't get shot up."

A wry grin played over Josh's lips. "Not so lucky. Twice in the leg, once in the chest, and once in the arm."

So intent was the sheriff on Josh's story, he forgot about the cigarette between his fingers. Suddenly, he shouted and whipped his hand to the side, throwing away the cigarette butt that had burned his fingers.

Josh laughed. "Jasper can hurt himself like that, Sheriff."

"Reckon so," Rabb replied, growing serious. "Reckon a man can get hurt in a heap of ways, but I've never blamed a body for taking care of hisself." He looked deep into Josh's eyes and nodded.

"Thanks," was all Josh said, suddenly aware of just how much better he felt now that he had shared his guilt with someone else. He blew out through his lips, and like water coursing down through open sluice gates, words poured from his lips, spilling out his deepest thoughts. "Still, I have considered going back—figuring I'd feel better about myself, now and in the years to come."

The sheriff shrugged, and with a gruff voice replied. "I know the feeling, son." He paused, then added, "But, were it me, I'd probably reckon I had done a heap more than my share. Of course," he added. "Every manjack of us has got to make up his own mind."

Josh considered the old sheriff's words. He nodded. "I suppose you're right." He drew a deep breath and changed the subject. "Now, let's get back to important matters. What about McCool? What do you reckon he's up to?"

Twisting his mustache thoughtfully, Sheriff Rabb studied Josh several moments. "The man is too smart to sign his name to a forged document. I reckon we just got to keep our eyes open and keep digging. Maybe we'll get lucky."

"Maybe. And maybe we won't."

His eyes narrowing suspiciously, Lee Rohmann studied the faces staring at him from around the table. He cleared his throat. "Sunday is when we hit. The gold will be stored in the safe at the Wells Fargo. The church is planning a big hoorah, and while everyone is busy there, we'll slip in, take the gold from the safe, and be long gone before anyone knows what happened. In fact, they won't know it's missing until they open the strong box down in Houston."

"What do you mean?"

Rohmann nodded to a metal box in the corner of the room. Around the middle of the box was a padlocked steel strap. "That's the box they'll carry on to Houston. It is identical to the one the gold is in."

One of the conspirators snorted. "Suppose you tell us just how you plan on pulling off that little miracle. The Wells Fargo agent, Amos Dunlop, is the only one what can open the safe."

Rohmann sneered. "You think so, huh? Well, don't worry. We'll have that gold just like I said."

Chapter Sixteen

As Josh reined away from the hitching rail, Slick McCool stepped through the batwing doors onto the porch. He lit a thin cheroot and nodded to Josh. "Afternoon, deputy."

His voice chilly, Josh replied, "Howdy, McCool."

The lean saloon owner gestured into the direction Josh was heading. "That shack of mine still keeping the weather off your head?"

"So far."

McCool chuckled and stepped back inside the saloon.

As Josh rode south out of town, Sonora Fats and his hardcases rode in from the west and pulled up in front of the saloon.

Grat Plummer climbed down off his pony and

stomped into the saloon. "I reckon I sure got me a big thirst for a bottle of that tonsil varnish McCool puts out."

Mike Gray-Eyes ambled out to the small barn while Josh unsaddled and tended Buck. He spotted the raw wound on the side of Josh's head. "You find trouble," he muttered.

"Yeah." He touched his fingers to the wound. "Close."

The old Kickapoo said nothing, but Josh knew what was on the old Indian's mind. "All right. Soon as I grain Buck, I'll come inside and tell you the whole story."

The shack was warm and dry, and Mike Gray-Eyes had boiled up a pot of rabbit stew. While Josh put himself around two heaping bowls of the thick stew filled with chunks of rabbit and bulbs of the *camote de raton,* what the Kickapoos called the mouse's sweet potato, he filled the old Indian in on all that had taken place.

Mike Gray-Eyes grunted when Josh finished. "Day after you leave, I hunt in snow. I see man who handles white-man's writing leave preacher's big house. Soon preacher leave." He extended his thin arm to the north. "Ride into storm."

Josh pondered the new information. The preacher and the postmaster. Nothing unusual about them meeting except maybe in the middle of a snowstorm. Why such urgency? Could it have been something between the two that sent Reverend Adams to Lee Rohmann's shack?

Outside, a cold October night settled over Junction

Flats. Off to the icy north, cold stars glittered, and a coyote howled, sending shivers down Josh's spine.

Josh had awakened around midnight. Unanswered questions tumbled about in his head. With a groan, he rose, stoked the fire, and tried to make sense of the events of the last few days.

"Here's how I see it, Sheriff," he said next morning as he poured a cup of steaming coffee. "McCool's name is on the bill of sale for the rustled cattle. The more I thought about it last night, the more skeptical it made me. It don't make sense. With what he takes in at the saloon, I'd figure he makes enough to buy up land hereabouts, even the Windham spread. So why jump into something as chancy as rustling? And I keep coming back to the foolishness of signing his own name to the bills of sale."

Sheriff Rabb shrugged. "Greed. It can turn even a good man every which way but loose."

"Maybe so, but let's find out just how much McCool's worth. Can't you talk to the banker? You've known him all your life."

An hour later, Josh listened with mixed feelings as J.T. Brachman, owner of Junction Flats First State Bank of Texas, frowned and remarked, "You're not serious, are you, August? You know I'm not at the liberty to discuss the personal affairs of my customers."

Sheriff Rabb snorted and shifted his splinted leg

around on the chair to ease the discomfort. "Blast it, J.T. I hobbled all the way over here to save time. Now, I could get the judge to sign an order, and he'd sign it. You know that. I know that. Then I'd bring it back here, and you'd have to do just what I'm asking you to do now. So, let's just save ourselves a heap of time, and you tell me what I want to know."

The banker sighed and blew out through his lips in resignation. "First, tell me exactly what you want to know, and then we'll see."

"Not much at all, Mr. Brackman," Josh replied. "McCool bought a spread south of town where I'm staying and the Windham place back north. Now, we don't care how much they cost. All we want to know is if McCool had trouble raising the money to buy the two spreads."

The banker studied them shrewdly, the replied, "He didn't walk in and plop down cash, if that's what you wondered." He paused, eyed them warily once again. "And I think that's exactly what you wanted to know, August John. I'm no fool. I hear of the rustling going on outside of Kimble County. You must figure McCool has a hand in it, probably because of the business he runs." He shrugged. "Well, I don't know about that. And as far as I know, he might have a roomful of greenbacks hidden away, but I doubt it. The truth is, I'm carrying McCool's note on the two spreads. He makes his payments regular. And those times trail herds push through, and he picks up extra cash, he puts it against the principal. That and the beef he sells to Fort McKavett just keeps him afloat." He grunted. "Wish all my customers were as conscientious as Mr. McCool. He might run a saloon and sell Demon Rum, but he's a sound businessman who knows what he wants and makes the necessary sacrifices to get it." J.T. Brackman hesitated, then added. "Off the record, Sheriff. If McCool's luck doesn't change, he could lose both spreads."

Sheriff Rabb frowned. "That ain't what I expected to hear, J.T."

"Expected or not, Sheriff. That's the truth in it."

Josh cleared his throat. "Did you say that McCool sells beef to Fort McKavett, J.T.?"

The banker nodded. "It's no secret. He buys up stock from surrounding counties when he can and sells the army beef. Perfectly legitimate."

Slogging through the mud on the way back to the jail, Josh grunted. "Well, McCool don't sound like any rustler to me. More like an enterprising businessman."

"Maybe not, but then, he's always hanging around Sonora Fats and his bunch."

"Correction, Sheriff. They're always hanging around his saloon."

"Same thing. What is it they say, mess with a skunk and you're going to stink?"

Josh opened the jailhouse door and with a wry grin, waited for the sheriff to enter. "I never heard that. Besides, I thought you didn't have anything on Sonora Fats?"

"I don't. Not here in Kimble County. That's what

galls me raw when him and his boys ride in big as life. I can't touch them, and none of the law in the other counties have asked for my help, and they won't." He turned to face Josh. "Fats is rustling. I'm convinced of that, but I figure he pays off the law in the other counties, so they look the other way."

"We have any proof he's doing the rustling?"

With a look of defeat on his face, Sheriff Rabb shook his head. "No."

Josh closed the door behind him. With a rueful grin, he said. "What it amounts to we can't go after Fats in the other counties because we'd be breaking the law we're sworn to uphold."

Sheriff Rabb plopped down in his swivel chair behind the desk. "Afraid so."

Josh studied the sheriff several moments. It made no sense, the law tying the hands of those trying to stop the rustling, but he kept his thoughts to himself. He stared out the window at the muddy street.

After a moment, the sheriff added. "You know, Josh, those hombres that shot you might have been Fat's old boys. You might have stumbled on to his hideout up north."

At that moment, the door swung open, and Doc Sears strode in. He plopped his black satchel down on the table and gestured for Josh to sit in the chair in front of the desk. "Let's have a gander at that head, Deputy. Got to make sure you're in good health for the box dinner tomorrow."

"Thanks for looking after me, Doc," Josh growled.

"Part of the service," the old physician joked, winking at Sheriff Rabb. "Want to make sure you got the energy to stay up with that pretty little Simmons gal."

"Just take care of my head, Doc. Save the comments, all right?"

While the doc chuckled and tended his head, Josh decided that he needed to find out if in fact the Circle B and the Flying W had sold stock to McCool. The ranches in the other counties could wait. Then he would have a talk with the dapper saloon owner. Afterward, he could ride out to Fort Terrett and see if there were any trace of the Simmons's herd.

Late that night after the town had gone to bed, a patrol of fourteen Confederates rode into Junction Flats, reining up in front of the Wells Fargo. The light in Wells Fargo came on, and four of the young cavalry boys hauled a padlocked box inside.

Leaving sentries front and back, the captain ordered his corporal to quarter the patrol at the local hotel for the night while he awakened the sheriff to inform him of the Confederate gold stored in his town.

Sheriff Rabb whistled softly when Josh rode in next morning. "Looks like someone got hisself all spiffed up for the box dinner social." He grinned.

Decked out in a new set of duds and slicked down hair, Josh grinned sheepishly. "Well, Miss Mary's been after me for the last two weeks to buy her box. Maybe if I do, she'll leave me be."

Shaking his head slowly, the sheriff muttered, "You just don't know beans about women, boy. Nothing at all, do you?" And then he grew serious, filling Josh in on the shipment of gold. "The army's keeping sentries, but it might not hurt for us to keep an eye out. The captain said nobody knew about the gold, but I don't much trust that. Gold has got a way of letting everyone know it's around."

Josh rubbed the back of his neck, pushing his plan to visit with McCool aside while the gold was in town. "I'll be mighty glad when that gold is gone. How much is it?"

Sheriff Rabb shook his head. "The captain didn't say."

Under his breath, Josh muttered a short prayer.

Chapter Seventeen

Next morning, Corporal Joseph Poole paused in the arched door that opened into the dining parlor of the Cattleman's Hotel and scanned the room for Captain Edgars. The career soldier's eyes fell on the captain near a window and strode smartly across the room.

He snapped to attention and delivered a crisp salute. "Excuse me, Captain. The local church is having a box dinner after morning services today. Raising money for schoolbooks. The men respectfully request permission to attend church and the box dinner afterward."

The captain arched an eyebrow. "What about sentry duty at Wells Fargo?"

"You've seen the roster, sir. I made it a point to post Private Brooks in front of Wells Fargo and me at the rear post during church services and the box dinner, if that's all right with the captain."

Captain Edgars leaned back in his chair at the breakfast table. He sucked on a tooth and grimaced. "I'd much prefer riding on today, Corporal. The weather's accommodating, and we'd be another day closer to our destination, but our orders are to remain here and leave tomorrow, so that's what'll we'll do." He nodded. "Permission granted. Carry on."

Upstairs a few minutes later, Corporal Poole peered out the window of his second floor room into the forest of scrub oak surrounding Junction Flats. From his vantage point, he saw that most of the snow had melted, a distinct advantage for the thin consistency of the mud would hold no sign for more than a few minutes, if that long.

A flash of light caught his attention. He raised and lowered the window shade twice in response.

In the forest, Lee Rohmann hurried back deep into the rugged hills and mesas to the small group of five Yankee sympathizers, Copperheads by southern definition, patriots by northern thinking.

They had camped in a rocky bower, the top of which was overshadowed by precipices of limestone through which smoke from the campfire filtered, breaking it apart, and losing it forever.

The five looked up when Rohmann rode in. He dismounted and reached for the coffee. "Two o'clock. That's when we hit."

* * *

From where he was crouched behind an ancient mesquite, Mike Gray-Eyes remained motionless, studying the small cluster of men, curious as to the meaning of the words he had just overheard. He wondered if Josh would understand what they meant. Probably not, the old Kickapoo told himself. The young today seemed to possess the brains of a bullfrog. He looked up into the blue heavens, searching for guidance.

The sound of an approaching rider caused the old warrior to press up against the rugged bark of the mesquite. He peered through a tangle of branches and spotted the 'the-one-who-handles-white-man's-writing.'

He turned to slip away, but his crutch punched through the crust on the snow down into a rabbit hole, causing the old man to lose his balance and crash into a small shrub. The snapping of the branches sounded like gunfire.

"What was that?" One of the Copperheads exclaimed, jumping to his feet and peering in the direction of the commotion.

"What? I didn't hear nothing."

"Well, I did," said the first, shucking his six-gun and disappearing into the woods.

The bright sun had melted the snow except for a few patches deep in the shadows cast by the buildings about town. Main Street was ankle deep in mud and limestone cobbles, and most of the ladies attending church and the box dinner afterward either reached the church on buckboards or along the temporary wooden walks that men of the church had lain across the muddy street.

Several soldiers of the Confederate patrol joined in the Sunday services and eagerly anticipated bidding against the local gents for the privilege of dining with one of the fair young ladies of the village.

And the extra competition for their boxes caused Junction Flats' young ladies to break into excited giggles.

As the last notes of the final church hymn died away, Sheriff Rabb grinned at Josh. "Sounds like church is over. Reckon it's time for the box dinner, don't you think?"

Josh ignored the good-natured jibing. "Sure sounds that way." With a sigh, he rose, tugged his hat down over his slicked-down hair and headed out the door, reminding himself to learn if the Circle B and Flying W had sold beef to McCool. "See you later."

"Save me a piece of chicken," the sheriff called after Josh, laughing at his young deputy's discomfort. "And don't forget. She tied it up with a yellow ribbon."

Josh ignored him.

The white clapboard church was more crowded than a dozen cowpokes in a single bunk. At either end of the sanctuary, pot-bellied stoves gleamed red hot, driving out the biting chill left by the late October storm.

Josh's eyes popped open when he spotted over two dozen gaily wrapped boxes sitting on tables in front of the altar, half of them tied up with yellow ribbons.

Against the west wall was another row of tables heaped with various meats and vegetables and sweet dishes supplied by ladies of the town and intended for those unfortunates unable to win a bid for one of the coveted box dinners.

The deputy caught his breath when he saw Mary Simmons in the church sanctuary. With a lacy bonnet perched on the back of her blond head, she wore a crisply starched blue gingham dress cinched in at her narrow waist. She beamed brightly at him. Awkwardly, he removed his hat as she hurried to him.

While he had seen her in a dress or two, he was still surprised at just how fine a picture she made all decked out in such dainty feminine garb. Then, he had to suppress a grin when he spotted the toe of her boot peek out from her the hem of her dress.

She held out her hand as she came up to him. "Hello, Josh."

He nodded. "Miss Mary. You—you look right nice."

Smiling demurely, she dropped her gaze to the floor. "In this old thing. Why thank you, Josh. You are truly a gentleman." She seized his hand. "Now, come over and say hello to Pa and the boys."

To Josh's disbelief, Ed and Hamm sat in a pew along with their brother and father. All four grinned at Josh. "Surprised to see you boys," he said as they shook hands.

"Not as surprised as we are to be here." Ed laughed.

Hamm joined in. "That goes double for me."

Arch Simmons spoke up. "I don't exactly know what's in that medicine that Injun friend of yours gave these boys, but I'd swear I can see the skin healing up right before my eyes."

Hamm spoke up. "What is in it? You know?"

Josh shrugged. "All Mike said was a ground-up mixture of cottonwood and butternut bark."

Mary slid her arm through Josh's and hugged up against his arm.

"Lordy, lordy. Never would have figured something like that. Truth is, Josh," said Hamm sheepishly. "I never cared for redstic—I mean Injuns before, but this old man has sure done me and Ed here a heap of good."

"And without asking for nothing in payback," Arch Simmons added wryly.

"Yeah. He ain't asked for nothing. And we'd like to do something for him," Ed explained.

Josh chuckled. "Mike Gray-Eyes has got all he wants. But, I'll pass word on. He'll be right obliged at the good thoughts."

At that moment, Reverend Adams stepped into the pulpit and held up his hand for silence. "Just a reminder to all, after the dinner, we'll have a social hour of games for all who would like to remain and participate."

In the midst of shouts of approval and several hoorahs, he turned the proceedings over to Louise Acincourt Tyler, the local school marm, who thanked all for participating in the schoolbook fundraiser. "Now, ladies and gentlemen, Mr. Lester Boles, our honorable post master, will serve as auctioneer." With a wide smile on her face, she added, "So, bid high. The school needs textbooks for your children."

And then amid laughter and excited exclamations, the lively bidding began, spirited and animated. Some of the younger crowd, emboldened by repeated pulls from concealed bottles of various snake poisons, was raucous, but good-natured, remembering just where they were.

Josh leaned toward Mary and whispered. "There's a heap of boxes with yellow ribbons, Miss Mary."

She laughed softly. "Don't worry. I'll tell you which one."

Archer elbowed Josh. "Come with me," he said. "We still got plenty time before Mary's box comes up."

Josh frowned at Mary who smiled and nodded. "Go on," she whispered, the knowing smile on her face dimpling her cheeks.

Followed by Hamm and Kelt, he headed down the hall beside the chancel, the same hall from which Josh had noticed several grinning townsmen coming and going

Out behind the church, Josh discovered another table, this one loaded with bottles of moonshine as well as store bought whisky. Archer poured a couple fingers in some tin mugs, then held one up for a toast. "To the Injun."

They all joined in.

Josh grinned at Archer and the boys, and a warm feeling glowed in his chest, and he knew it wasn't from the whiskey.

"Got any of that snake poison left?"

Josh looked around as Hank Bartholomew closed the door behind him.

"Hello, Hank," Arch Simmons roared. "Why, believe it or not, we left a bottle just for you."

The old rancher downed a gulp, then patted his belly. "Hits the spot."

Arch grew serious. "Hear you're sending a herd down to Kerrville."

Bartholomew frowned. "Where'd you hear that?' He asked suspiciously."

"The preacher." Arch pointed the tin cup toward the church. "He told us back inside a few minutes ago."

Bartholomew grinned and relaxed. "You scared me there. I thought word had got out."

"Nope. Just the preacher."

Downing another gulp, the old rancher nodded. "Got to get me some cash for the winter. If I don't—" H paused and blew out through his lips. "Well—"

Arch Simmons grew somber. "I know, Hank. I know."

Josh saw his opportunity. "What about McCool? Won't he buy them?"

Unperturbed by the question, the old rancher shook his head. "I done asked. He ain't got the money this time."

Nodding slowly, Josh started to let the matter drop. He had learned what he wanted. McCool's sales to the Army appeared legitimate, but he posed one further question. "Do others around here sell to McCool?"

Archer Simmons broke in. "Some do. He's wanted to buy some of mine, but I ain't been hard up enough to give my beef away."

"That ain't fair, Arch," Bartholomew snapped. "You got to give a man some profit for driving stock all the way to McKavett."

Back inside, the bidding moved along rapidly, and to Josh's chagrin, he had to battle through a formidable bidding war for Mary's box with two Confederate cavalry boys and a middle aged widower looking for a wife for himself and a mother for his two girls.

Josh won the box for sixteen dollars and twenty-five cents. "I was down to my last dollar," he whispered to Mary as they opened the box on the table between them.

"No need to worry. I would have given you all of the money you needed," she replied, laughing shamelessly at her own brazen response.

Couples squeezed in beside Josh and Mary until they were all shoulder-to-shoulder. "Tell you what," Josh said, standing up and loading the food back into the box. "Let's take this over to the jail and share it with the sheriff. I'll tell your Pa."

Moments later, they were making their way over the uncertain boards spanning the lakes of mud until finally they reached McCool's Saloon where Josh, and surprisingly not as much to his displeasure as he would have imagined, carried Mary across the muddy street to the jail.

She was light as baking soda biscuits. Why, Josh told himself, there's no telling how far I could carry her.

Mary simply smiled demurely up at him.

* * *

Inside, Sheriff Rabb grinned like a lobo wolf eyeing a helpless cottontail as he put himself around the fried chicken, new potatoes, sourdough biscuits, fresh churned butter, and chocolate cake. Accompanied with a pot of fresh coffee, the meal was a dandy repast.

Throughout the meal, Mary kept looking up at Josh, smiling as if expecting him to say something, and when he kept telling her just how tasty her grub was, she seemed disappointed.

Sheriff Rabb saw what was taking place, but he said nothing. The only time he opened his mouth was to poke another chunk of grub between his lips.

Josh had planned to tell the sheriff of the legitimacy of McCool's cattle deals, but he decided to wait until they were alone. A few minutes later, a faint knock sounded at the rear door. Josh frowned at the sheriff. "You hear something?"

Before he could answer, another knock sounded. Josh hurried to the back door.

"Mike!" He exclaimed when he saw the old Kickapoo, soaking wet and covered with mud, sagging up against the doorjamb, blood running down his face from an ugly cut on his forehead. "What the Sam Hill—" quickly, he crouched beside the old man and slipped an arm around his chest. "Let's get you in here."

Mary hurried to the door and jerked to a halt when she saw the old Kickapoo. "What—good Lord." She got on the other side of Mike Gray-Eyes, ignoring the mud and water.

"Let's get him on the bunk in the cell," Josh said.

"Sheriff, get him some hot coffee and a slug of whiskey."

They sat the old man on the bunk and tried to force a cup of coffee through his lips, but the hot liquid ran down the sides of his lips. "What the blazes happened to you, Mike?"

The old Kickapoo's lips trembled. He held up two trembling fingers and muttered a single word, "writing", and then his entire body shivered, and he went limp.

Uttering one curse after another, Josh quickly stripped the wet and muddy rags from the old Indian and wrapped him in several blankets. Finally, he rose to his feet and stared down at his old friend.

"What do you reckon happened?" Sheriff Rabb remarked.

Josh shook his head. "He was soaked. If I didn't know the old man better, I'd say he fell into the Llano River out there, but even crippled up like he is, he wouldn't do that."

Mary looked up at him. "So what is going on? What did he mean by 'writing' or holding up two fingers?"

All Josh could do was stare at the unconscious old Indian whose breathing was becoming labored. "I got no idea, but I need the doctor over here."

Josh found Doc Sears at the church with Reverend Adams. "He's in bad shape, Doc. I don't know what happened to him. He's got a bad cut on his head. He's an old man. He was soaked to the bone and covered

with mud. Somewhere, he lost his crutch, so no telling
how far he crawled on his hands and knees. A shock
like this might do him in. He's unconscious right now,
and I think his breathing's growing worse."

Lester Boles came up behind Reverend Adams as the
preacher watched the deputy and the doctor stride down
the street. Boles leaned forward and whispered, "We
need to talk."

A look of impatience flickered over the minister's
face, but he nodded to the rear. "My office."

His office was at the end of the hall adjacent to the
choir pit. The office was small with a desk, a bookcase
and two chairs against the second wall, and a stove next
to the third. A door on the fourth wall opened into a
closet.

Reverend Adams closed the office door behind them
and demanded. "Now what's so blasted important for
you to take a chance like this?"

Boles explained. "What the deputy was saying. That
must be the commotion we heard this morning."

Adams looked down at the smaller man in disbelief.
"What?"

"I told you. Just as I rode in this morning, Rohmann
and the others claimed they heard someone out in the
woods. They went out searching, but didn't find nothing. It mighta been that old man."

The preacher muttered a curse. His eyes narrowed.

Boles whined. "So, what about the sixty-thousand?
We still taking it?"

Adams glanced at the Regulator clock on the wall, its

pendulum clicking back and forth. "It's one-thirty. We've gone too far to back out now." He paused and drew a deep breath. "We'll stay with the plan. If nothing goes wrong, the gold will be in Huntsville within two or three days. We'll get our twenty-five percent and keep the rest there until it's safe to transport it on down to Galveston."

"What if the old Injun wakes up?"

Adams drew a deep breath and released it slowly. "We'll worry about that when and if it happens. Now, let's get back out front."

After the door closed, the closet door across the room creaked open. Sonora Fats looked out, a satisfied sneer on his face. He had ridden in to pay his brother a visit, and the hypocritical little traitor had provided him with much more than he anticipated.

Moving quietly, he slipped out the back door. He'd return later, when he could be alone with his brother. Sonora Fats shook his head at the irony of what he had just learned. He admitted that he himself was nothing more than a ordinary, thieving rustler, but his holier-than-thou little brother was worse by far. He was not only breaking God's law by pretending to be a preacher, but he was also a traitor to the Confederate cause.

Chapter Eighteen

Doc Sears grimaced when he saw Mike Gray-Eyes lying on the bunk. The old Kickapoo warrior looked like nothing more than a strip of blackened beef jerky wrapped in blankets. "This old man can't weigh anymore than a hundred pounds," he muttered as he checked the pulse in the Mike's thin wrist. "Umm, weak, but fairly steady. That's a surprise." He checked the ugly wound on the old man's forehead. "Looks like he fell and hit a rock or something." He glanced over his shoulder at Josh. "He needs hot liquids—soup, stew, whatever you can get down him."

Mary moved quickly and efficiently. "Hot soup it is," she replied, using the hem of her dress to wipe out a dusty saucepan she found hanging on the jailhouse wall and banging it down on the hot stove. She splashed a couple dipperfuls of water in the pan and began mashing the leftover new potatoes from her box dinner. She grinned up at Josh. "Hope you don't mind. You paid for them."

"Not one bit," Josh answered, opening the door on the pot-bellied stove and tossing in three more split logs.

Doc Sears finished examining the old Indian. He grinned crookedly. "He's unconscious now. See if you can get a few swallows down his gullet anyway. Enough so he'll get some good sleep. He looks plumb tuckered out. I'm surprised at how he's handling this, especially for an old man. I just hope I'm in as good a shape as he is when I get to be that age." He looked up at Josh. "How old do you reckon he is?"

"With Indians, you can't tell. From stories I heard from him, I'd have to reckon in his eighties or older."

Sheriff Rabb whistled softly.

Josh nodded. "Once, he told me that when he was a young boy, he heard his father and others in the tribe discussing the war back east with the redcoats. Anyway you cut the deck, that's eighty or so years ago."

The doctor slipped back into his coat and buttoned it against the cold. "Well, that's all I can do. Feed him good and keep him warm." He licked his lips and eyed the boiling water that was quickly turning the mashed potatoes into a thick, tasty potato stew. "Smells good, Mary."

She blushed. "Come out to the house anytime, Doc. I'll whip you up a batch."

He winked at Josh. "You best grab her up, son, or I might just beat you to her."

Josh turned crimson and muttered a few unintelligible words.

Mary beamed.

Doc noticed the second cell was empty. "What happened to them two galoots that tried to hold up Luddy at the general store?"

Sheriff Rabb hooked his thumb back to the east. "On the way to Huntsville Prison."

Outside, Doc Sears stood on the boardwalk, looking up and down the nearly deserted street of the small town. At the north end of the street, laughter and music echoed from the church. He grinned. One thing about this preacher, he wasn't one of those so stuck up in his religion that he wouldn't permit good music and laughter.

Whistling a rousing chorus of *Darling Clementine*, Doc Sears stepped off the boardwalk and sloshed across the muddy street, anxious to return to the conviviality of the box dinner.

Corporal Joseph Poole looked around at the sharp whistle. A figure stood just inside the line of scrub oak behind the saloon. He glanced between the Wells Fargo building and the post office next door. There had been no traffic on the boardwalk for the last hour or so. Private Brooks would be standing directly in front of the Wells Fargo door. He drew a deep breath. Now was the time.

Without taking his eyes off the corridor between the

two buildings just in case the private suddenly
appeared, Corporal Poole waved the all clear signal to
the figure on the edge of the forest.

Moments later, footsteps sloshed through the mud
behind him. He signaled for them to move faster. He
looked around briefly and saw Lee Rohmann. He
growled. "You got two minutes."

Rohmann nodded and quickly climbed the rear steps
and unlocked the door. He stood aside as four men hurried inside, two of them lugging a metal chest with a
steel band padlocked around the middle of the chest.

He hurried inside behind them and eased the door
shut.

Corporal Poole breathed easier. Mentally, he ticked
off the seconds. At ninety seconds, the door opened.
Rohmann looked out. Poole stayed him a moment until
all was clear, then waved them out.

Moving briskly, four of the five Copperheads, two of
them lugging a chest identical to the one they had just
carried inside, hurried back to the forest where the
remaining Yankee sympathizer was holding the horses.
Rohmann remained inside, locking the safe.

At that moment, a voice from the corridor between
the two buildings jerked Corporal Poole around. He
froze when he spotted Doc Sears making his way down
between the two buildings.

Forcing himself to remain calm, Corporal Poole
glanced at the retreating men. They were still several
yards from the shelter of the scrub oak, a distance too
far to cover before the doctor emerged from between

the two buildings. Poole stepped forward, blocking the doctor's progress. "Sorry, Sir. Citizens aren't permitted back here."

At that moment, Lee Rohmann clambered down the steps, closing the door behind him. "There," he announced. "That does—" His words caught in his throat when he spotted Doc Sears. "Doc—" he managed to choke out, his eyes wide with surprise.

Sears frowned up at Rohmann on the rear steps of the Wells Fargo, then looked at the corporal. He glanced to his right just as the four jaspers disappeared into the forest. "Who are those men? What are they carrying? Rohmann, what the blazes is going on here?" He demanded, jerking back around to glare at the smaller man, but all he saw was the butt of a Sharps rifle just before it crushed the front of his skull.

Poole and Rohmann dragged Doc Sears through the mud and left him beneath the post office. The corporal tossed the doctor's black bag beside the dead man. "Get some help to carry him out of here," the corporal ordered the smaller man. "Hide the body back in the forest somewhere."

Rohmann glanced nervously at the post office. "What about Boles?"

"Boles?" Corporal Poole frowned.

"Yeah. The postmaster. He's one of us."

Poole considered the question only a moment before replying. "Tell him nothing. Let it be as big a surprise to him as the rest of the town."

Rohmann nodded and quickly hurried after the others. Corporal Poole watched the small man scurry into the woods. He looked at the body under the post office and muttered a curse. The town doctor. Why the Sam Hill couldn't it have been someone else? There was no way the town sawbones would not be missed.

For the next ten minutes, Corporal Poole held his breath, expecting discovery at any moment, but to his relief, four sympathizers hurriedly carried the old doctor's corpse away, and Poole spent the next forty-five minutes marching up and down on his post, obliterating the tracks of the Copperheads with his own before his relief arrived.

Later that afternoon, Archer Simmons pulled up in front of the jail in his surrey with Hamm and Ed in the back seat. Kelt rode alongside on a nervous blood bay.

The old rancher lumbered inside, his cheeks laced with tiny pink capillaries and his nose red from too much celebrating and not enough eating. "Come along now, Mary Honey. Time to get back. Give these gents time to do their jobs." He laughed, and then a frown knit his brow. "Where's Doc? I don't see him around."

Josh and the sheriff exchanged puzzled looks. "Doc? Lordy, Arch, you must've been gulping too much of that snake poison if you missed him. He left here a couple hours back. Heading back to the church social."

Archer Simmons frowned, pursed his lips thoughtfully, then shook his head emphatically. "He wasn't back at the church. I'd swear that." He opened the door and shouted. "Hey, boys. Any of you see Doc Sears the last couple hours back at the church?"

As one they shook their heads.

Mary spoke up. "Maybe he stopped off to see a patient."

"Maybe." Josh shrugged. "Or one of those soldier-boys might have took sick." He hesitated, a nagging worry suddenly bristling the hair on the back of his neck.

"Well, he'll show up," Sheriff Rabb announced. "Old Doc always does."

Arch Simmons grunted. "Yep, reckon you're right, August John. Well, come along, little girl. We best get before dark."

"All right, Pa," Mary replied, standing and brushing at the skirt of her blue gingham dress. She glanced at the floor, waiting.

Josh stood and cleared his throat.

Behind them, Sheriff Rabb grinned and winked at Archer Simmons.

"I . . . I sure enjoyed today, Miss Mary," Josh stammered. "The grub—I mean, the food was right tasty."

She smiled up at him shyly. "I'm right glad you liked it, Josh. You're welcome anytime."

He nodded awkwardly, struggling for words that refused to come.

Archer Simmons cleared his throat and grinned at the sheriff.

Mary shot her Pa a look rimmed with fire, then

looked back up at Josh. After a moment, she realized the lanky deputy was entirely too shy to make the first move, so impulsively, she stood on tiptoe, touched her lips to his weathered cheek, and raced out the door.

Josh's ears burned as the old rancher shut the door behind them. Josh glared at Sheriff Rabb, daring him to utter a single word. The sheriff leaned back in his chair and built a cigarette, all the while with a straight face whistling a shaky rendition of *Here Comes the Bride*.

Later, as the sun dropped behind the western horizon, Josh rose and stretched. "Reckon if you got no objection, Sheriff, me and Mike will sleep here tonight. You might as well go back to your room at the hotel for a good night's sleep."

August Rabb grunted. "Blazes, son, I ain't had a good night's sleep in years. Reckon I'd as soon as sack out on a bunk in one of the cells as to hobble through the mud to the hotel." A expression of concern filled his eyes. "Besides, I didn't let on earlier, but I'm worried about Doc. Why don't you do me a favor, Josh, and see if you can run that old rascal down. I'd sleep better tonight. I'll look after your Injun friend while you're gone."

"You bet. Oh, by the way. I talked to Hank Bartholomew at the church. Seems McCool has bought cows from him to sell up at Fort McKavett like the banker said."

Sheriff Rabb arched a quizzical eyebrow. "You didn't believe J.T.?"

Josh grinned sheepishly. "Just wanted a second opinion, Sheriff. Just wanted a second opinion," he replied, slipping into his heavy woolen Mackinaw. "See you later."

Josh slugged through the mud to the saloon, figuring on starting his search there for Doc Sears had never made any excuses of his love for good bourbon.

Half-a-dozen Confederate cavalry sat around one table, laughing and joking, while three or four citizens bellied up to the bar. Three big pot-bellied stoves heated the large room.

McCool stood behind the shiny bar with the brass foot rail.

"Evening, Deputy. What's brings you here?" He wiped at the slick bar. "Things have been mighty quiet since the cavalry come to town. How about a beer?"

Josh leaned an elbow on the bar. "Might as well, a short one. I been out looking for old Doc Sears."

McCool slid the beer down the bar. "Hadn't seen him today. Just a minute. I did see him, around two or three. He was coming out of the jail and headed down the boardwalk in front here, heading toward the church. Figured he was going back to the party."

"That's what I figured too. You should have joined us up there at the church. Folks had a dandy time."

McCool snorted and with a wry grin, said, "Me? A church social? Reckon I would have ruined it for most of those folks. After all, running a saloon ain't one of the most respected jobs around."

"Well, some might say it's not respectable, but at

least, you're honest. I never heard any jasper complain about crooked games in your place."

McCool hesitated and stared at Josh in disbelief. A crooked grin curled one side of his lips. "Well, Deputy, that's mighty white of you to say that, and I'm right pleased to hear folks know I run a respectable establishment here. Truth is, I got a history that's dark in places, but I paid my time before I came here, and I swore that if I had to buy up half the state, I was going to be respectable." He paused, and with a wry arch to his eyebrows, added. "Of course, between you and me, it's going to take a heap longer than I figured to buy up even a tad of that much."

Eyeing McCool, Josh sipped his beer. "Hear you're in the cattle business too."

The saloon owner shrugged, unfazed by the question. "When I have extra cash, and when the locals will sell."

"You don't run any stock yourself?"

He shook his head. "Last year, I bought the Windham spread back north of town. I wanted to run some stock out there, but it's up in Mason County, and them rustlers been working mighty hard up there. I learned I could make a little profit buying cows cheap and selling them high to the army."

"Not bad."

He grinned. "Risky, but so far, I hadn't been hit by the rustlers. Sent a small batch up just last week."

Josh drained the beer and chuckled. "Somehow,

McCool, I can't picture your forking a pony all the way up to Fort McKavett."

The dapper gambler laughed. "Not me. Sonora Fats pushes them up there for me." He hesitated, a crooked grin spreading over his lips. "Selman used to help until you buried him."

Frowning Josh remarked, "Kinda of a rough crowd you're trusting you stock with, ain't it?"

McCool paused in wiping the bar. "They were the only ones I could hire, Deputy. No one else would work for me. And I ain't lost a single head on the way."

"How do you handle it, I mean the bill of sale for the cattle if you don't go with the herd?"

"I sent it with Selman."

Josh nodded and gestured to the saloon. "You hear a lot of talk in here. Any idea about who's behind the rustling?"

McCool studied him, then leaned forward. "That's what's odd about the whole thing. Saloons are where deals like that are put together, but the truth is, I've not heard a word about the rustling other than those from out of county who've been hit. I got nothing to go on."

Nodding slowly, Josh replied, "I understand, but if you had to guess, who would you say was behind the rustling in the other counties?"

A faint sneer curled the saloon owner's lips. "Who do you think?"

"You're taking chances, aren't you?"

"No. I don't think so. Like the old saying, rats know where to go for the good corn."

Josh grinned. Their eyes met, and an understanding passed between the two.

McCool gave the bar a final wipe. "That's who I think also, Deputy."

Then an idea hit Josh. "McCool, how about making me a copy of that last bill of sale of yours you sent with Selman to Fort McKavett? Any trouble?"

The saloon owner shrugged. "No trouble. I'll have my bookkeeper make a copy and send it over to the jail."

"Much obliged." Josh touched his fingertips to the brim of his Stetson as he turned to leave.

At the same time Josh entered the saloon, Reverend Adams was standing in front of the church wishing the last family a safe trip home. He closed the door and headed back to his office.

"Howdy, Matt."

The preacher jerked around at the voice and froze when he saw his brother leering at him from the hallway beside the choir pit. "What are you doing here, Elm? Someone might see you." He hurried to his brother, closing the hall door behind them.

Feigning injured pride, Sonora Fats laughed. "Now, that ain't no decent way to greet your older brother."

Reverend Adams narrowed his eyes. "The Simmons' herd was rustled and one of the boys was shot up. You know anything about it?"

"Not a thing, Matt," Fats said in wide-eyed innocence. "I told you I was trying to go straight. My little
place out west of here ain't much, but I'm building it
up. That's why I'm here today. I got a little extra cash,
so I'm looking for some stock to buy. I figured this time
of year, some old boy might be hard up for cash, and I
could pick up a good deal."

Matthew Adams stared at his older brother, on the
one hand hoping he was trying to go straight, but on the
other resenting the position in which Elmer had put
him. Even though the side of his own furtive operation
had been completed, if anyone discovered that he and
Sonora Fats were brothers, the mission could still fail,
and such a possibility would continue to exist until the
gold was delivered to Union troops down on the coast
by Galveston.

He just wanted to be shed of Fats. "I reckon any
rancher hereabouts would be glad to sell some beeves.
I heard just this morning that Hank Bartholomew is
pushing a herd out tomorrow for Kerrville. He'll probably be right pleased to sell you beeves so he won't
have to trail them on down there."

Sonora Fats grinned, his fat lips turning almost
inside out. He slapped Matt on the shoulder. "Much
obliged, little brother. I'll see him about that first thing
in the morning." He paused when he heard a door close
in the sanctuary.

Chapter Nineteen

Josh stepped inside the empty sanctuary and closed the door behind him. "Reverend Adams! You around?"

The hallway door beside the choir pit opened slightly and the preacher peered out. He spotted Josh and called out, "Be right with you, Deputy." He closed the door, then opened it moments later.

Striding toward Josh with an amiable grin on his face, he held out his hand. "Evening, Deputy." And in a jovial manner, said, "I'm afraid we're all out of box dinners if that's what you're coming back for."

"Not tonight, Preacher." Josh laughed and took the preacher's extended hand. "I got my fill today. You had a nice crowd show up."

Reverend Adams agreed. "Life is hard out here, Deputy. Folks are always looking for a little fun and relaxation." He paused to toss a few split logs into the pot-bellied stove in anticipation of the evening service. "So, what can I do for you?"

At that moment, Josh glimpsed a horse and rider emerge from the rear of the church, but the deepening dusk made it difficult to recognize the rider as he rode off to the west. He shrugged it off. "Looking for Doc Sears."

Reverend Adams frowned. "He left here around one o'clock or so. Haven't seen him since. Someone need him?"

Josh shook his head. "No. Just trying to locate him. He's probably out making some calls," he replied, making a mental note to check the livery for the doctor's rig.

"Well, if I see him, I'll let him know you're looking for him."

Later at the jail, Josh stared down at the sheriff soberly. "Something's wrong, Sheriff. I couldn't find Doc anywhere in town. He left the church around one when he came down to the jail. His rigs still in the livery. Hasn't been out since Friday."

Rabb frowned. "That ain't like Doc."

"McCool was the last one to see him—around two or three this afternoon."

"McCool?"

"Yep. Said Doc was heading back toward the church."

The sheriff arched an eyebrow. "Maybe not."

"Maybe not? What do you mean?"

"I mean, McCool might not have been the last to see

Doc. The army—those cavalry boys. They been standing guard in front of Wells Fargo last night and all day today. If Doc was going down the boardwalk, one of them had to have spotted him."

Josh snapped his fingers. "Blast it, Sheriff. I'd forgotten all about them soldier boys." He headed for the door. "They're still over to the hotel. I'll talk to the captain."

"Oh, before you leave. McCool sent this to you."

"The bill of sale," Josh said, skimming down the document. A crooked grin played over his lips. It appeared his idea wasn't so far off as he thought.

Seeing a faint grin play over the deputy's lips, the sheriff asked. "Why the bill of sale?"

"Just a wild hunch, Sheriff. Probably nothing, but I reckon on paying Hank Bartholomew a visit tomorrow and then ride on up to Fort McKavett. Then I'll know for sure."

Fifteen miles into No-Mans Land, old Fort Terrett was a crumbling collection of limestone buildings caved in by years of neglect and weather, but it offered an ideal refuge and hideout for Sonora Fats and his gang of hardcases.

The owlhoots stabled their horses in the old infirmary next to the commissary where they bunked. Despite the state of disrepair, the two rooms were fairly solid, providing a snug shelter beyond the border of Kimble County, well outside of Sheriff August Rabb's authority to snoop.

When Sonora Fats stumbled in, Grat Plummer looked up from the poker game with Rowdy Joe Lowe and two drifters they'd picked up on their journey back from Fort McKavett after disposing of the Simmons' herd.

The four hardcases said nothing, simply watched warily as Fats turned up a bottle of rotgut whiskey, downed several gulps, then sliced off a chunk of beef broiling over the fire, which he promptly popped in his mouth and then wiped his greasy hand on his grease-caked trousers. He belched, downed another long drink of whiskey, and said. "We ride in the morning. I learned that old man Bartholomew is moving a herd down to Kerrville."

Plummer grunted. "They don't ever learn, do they?"

Fats eyed Plummer with amusement. "But that ain't where we're going."

Puzzled, Rowdy Joe Lowe leaned back in his chair and studied his boss. "What you got in mind?"

The idea of sixty thousand dollars clanked up bells in Sonora Fats' mind, but all he did was grin. "You'll see in the morning."

Corporal Joseph Poole snapped to attention and saluted smartly. "You wanted to see me, Captain?" He cut his eyes toward Josh who was standing beside Captain Edgar.

"Yes, Corporal. The deputy here is looking for Doc Sears. Seems the doctor just up and vanished today. He was last seen heading up the boardwalk from the saloon toward the church. That means he would have passed in front of Wells Fargo where we had stationed sentries."

The corporal stiffened imperceptibly, cursing under his breath. Just as he had figured, someone had missed the doctor. Luckily, the hour was late. By now, the gold had a four-hour head start. Come seven o'clock next morning, the patrol would move out. He cleared his throat. "Yes, Sir. What time are we looking at?"

Josh spoke up. "Around two o'clock, Corporal."

Without hesitation, Poole replied, "That would be Private Brooks, Captain. He was on duty in front of Wells Fargo from eleven o'clock to three. I was out back." He hesitated. Hoping to display just the right degree of curiosity, he asked. "By any chance, was the doctor an old man, Deputy?"

Josh grew alert. "About fifty or so. Wearing a black suit, carrying a black bag."

Poole looked at the captain. "Around that time, Captain, an old gentleman came down between the post office and Wells Fargo, and he was carrying a bag. I informed him he was not authorized to be back there, so he left. He headed north past the rear of the Wells Fargo and the building next to it."

"That's the general store. Ludwig Protkin's place," Josh explained.

The corporal nodded in deference to Josh's explanation. "I watched until the gentleman turned up between the buildings. Maybe Private Brooks saw him after that."

Private Brooks hadn't. "No, Sir. I did see him go down between the two buildings, but that was the last I saw of him."

"You didn't see him come back up on the boardwalk?"

"No, sir, but I could have been looking the other way when he came out."

Josh sloshed through the mud to the jail where he picked up a lantern and headed to the rear of Wells Fargo.

Corporal Poole hurried up to his room. Just as he reached for the doorknob, he froze, suddenly remembering the black bag the doctor had been carrying. Did Rohmann and the others pick it up when they carted off the dead man? Or was it still lying where Poole had tossed it under the post office?

He uttered a curse through clenched teeth and jerked open the door. He made his way through the darkened room to the window. Below, a lantern suddenly emerged between the two buildings, lighting the front of the sentry who was challenging the deputy. Poole chewed on his bottom lip, trying to imagine the conversation between the two.

Finally, the sentry stepped back, permitting Josh to peer at the ground in the rear of Wells Fargo, then slowly move to the north.

The mud behind Wells Fargo had been trampled by the patrolling sentries, but beyond the corner of the building were only a smattering of tracks, the age impossible to discern because of the thin consistency of the mud.

Josh peered into the corridors between the next three

buildings, the general store, the tonsorial parlor, and the milliner's, but he could find no sign of anyone passing through the patches of unmelted snow beneath the eaves.

At the milliner's, he cut back to the boardwalk.

A smug grin split Corporal Poole's face when the lantern light died away. Obviously, the deputy had found nothing, for there was nothing to be found. Or maybe, it being dark outside, the deputy overlooked something. The bag? He frowned. Maybe he should go down and look for himself. But what if someone saw him? How would he explain to the sentry on duty just what he was doing, what he was looking for?

On the other hand, the corporal told himself. If they discover the old man's body, the deputy will know I was lying.

"Beats the dickens out of me," Josh muttered, pouring a cup of coffee. He glanced at the sheriff who was sitting behind his desk, his broken leg resting on the rawhide seat of a straight back chair. "He hasn't been home. His housekeeper hasn't seen him since noon." Josh pointed the cup of steaming coffee at the sheriff, emphasizing his next remark. "I got a bad feeling something's happened, Sheriff. Something mighty bad."

The older man squinted up through the cigarette smoke, wrinkles forming deep grooves in his forehead. "Like what?"

Josh sighed. "I don't know. I honest-to-Pete don't

know." He hesitated and glanced curiously at the sheriff. "You don't think that—" He shook his head. "No. Couldn't be."

"What couldn't be?" Sheriff Rabb leaned forward, wincing as he shifted his injured leg.

The young deputy remained silent for several moments, stroking his chin thoughtfully as he tried to organize his thoughts. "All right, Sheriff, now maybe I'm stretching this higher than a sunfishing bronco, but other than the box dinner at church, the only thing different around here is the Confederate patrol and the gold. Now, you know Doc ain't good looking enough for any of those church women at the box dinner to take the notion to run off with him."

Sheriff Rabb chuckled. "Sure ain't none of them foolish enough to put up with the old codger."

The amusement faded from Josh's eyes. "So that leaves the gold."

For a moment, the older man pondered Josh's implication. "You think whatever happened to Doc Sears has something to do with the gold?" A faint edge of incredulity edged his words.

Josh grinned crookedly. "I don't know. All I'm saying is that the gold is the only thing different about Junction Flats."

For several seconds, the two stared at each other. Rabb cleared his throat. "What could he have found out that would have got him in trouble?"

Again Josh shook his head. He sipped the coffee, then set it on the stove while he built a Bull Durham.

"I'm making a fool out of myself so far, so I reckon I might as well do it up good and proper. What if the gold's gone? What if Doc stumbled on to a robbery? The corporal said he saw Doc go down between the milliner's and the tonsorial parlor. I couldn't find any tracks in the snow between the two buildings."

The sheriff arched a skeptical eyebrow. "The snow melted. Washed them all out."

"What about the patches where it hadn't melted? What if the snow didn't melt them? What if they were never made?" He touched the cigarette to the red-hot stovepipe to light it. "What if the gold is gone?"

"What about the army? The guards, the sentries?"

Josh blew out a stream of smoke. "They were part of it."

Momentarily speechless, the sheriff looked at Josh as if the younger man had been kicked in the head by a wild horse. Finally, he said, "That's loco thinking."

"Maybe so. You got a better suggestion?"

Sheriff Rabb shrugged. "What do you want to do?"

The young deputy shook his head. "I can't believe I'm saying this, but let's see if the gold is still there."

Chapter Twenty

Amos Dunlop, the Wells Fargo agent, protested all the way from his house on the outskirts of town to the front door of the agency where Captain Edgars and Corporal Poole were waiting.

By the glow of the lantern, he opened the door and led the way to the large safe in the rear of the room. "I'm the only one with keys to this safe. And I ain't taken nothing out. The gold's there, but if you've got to see, August John Rabb, then blast it, I'll let you see." He fumbled with a ring of keys, and unlocked a cold-rolled steel padlock. The heavy door swung open with drawn-out creak.

He stepped back. "There."

Corporal Joseph Poole held his breath.

Josh held the lantern forward. In the middle of the

safe sat a metal box with a thick iron band padlocked around its middle.

Captain Edgars spoke up, a trace of irritation in is words. "There's the box with gold, Sheriff. Satisfied?"

Josh stepped forward. "It was my idea, Captain. Sorry to put you to so much trouble."

Before he could reply, Amos Dunlop slammed the safe door and said, "Now, if everyone will leave so I can lock up, my dinner is getting cold."

The Confederate patrol moved out with the rising of the sun. Josh watched them ride out of town. In the first cell, Sheriff Rabb stirred. Josh paused in the door of the second. Mike Gray-Eyes still slept, but his breathing was regular and steady.

The young deputy had awakened hours before, and puzzled by the disappearance of Doc Sears, had been unable to go back to sleep. He made use of his time by fashioning the old Kickapoo another crutch, then bundling up in his Mackinaw and tugging his floppy hat down over his head, he ventured outside, the chilly air a welcome brace.

The small town was beginning to come to life. He wandered over to Josie's Café for a cup of coffee and a slab of apple pie, while he tried to sort through the puzzling events of the previous day.

"How's the pie, Josh?"

He looked up into the rotund face of Josie Whalen.

"As usual, Josie, mighty tasty. If you got anymore, I'll take a whole pie back to the sheriff."

She glanced out the window. "Looks like you won't have to do that. Here comes Sheriff Rabb now."

The look on the sheriff's face when he opened the café door told Josh the old lawman wasn't here for breakfast. "Josh. Get on back over to the jail. The old Kickapoo done woke up. I ain't sure, but you might not have been as wrong last night as we all figured."

Mike Gray-Eyes had slipped into his dry buckskins, and leaning on his new crutch, was nursing a cup of coffee when Josh and the sheriff returned.

"Tell him what you told me, Mike," Sheriff Rabb said, nodding to Josh.

The old Kickapoo grunted. "In woods, I hunt rabbit. Make stew. I see many men. There." He pointed east of town. "I hide. One white-eye say they do something at two o'clock, then man-who-white-people-give-writing come. They hear me. I run." He touched a bony finger to the ugly wound on his forehead. "Fall on rocks, then crawl through snow to river. Hide in cattails."

Sheriff Rabb frowned at Josh. "That's what he told me. What does he mean by it?"

Josh pondered his old friend's words. "The man-who-white-people-give-writing has to be Lester Boles, the post master. But two o'clock? I don't know." He shook his head, then snapped his fingers. "Unless— blast it! Wasn't it was around two when Doc disappeared?" He eyed the old Indian. "You saw the man-who-white-people-give-writing, huh?"

Mike grunted.

Josh pointed through the window at the post office. "That man?"

Mike grunted again.

Josh looked at the sheriff. "That's mighty peculiar. The postmaster shows up out there, and the post office is right next door to the Wells Fargo Agency." He pushed to his feet. "You two wait here. I want to pay the post office and the Wells Fargo another visit."

"What about Bartholomew and Fort McKavett?"

"Later."

Josh studied the ground at the rear of Wells Fargo and the post office, finding nothing to suggest what might have happened to Doc Sears. He knelt and peered beneath the two buildings. He saw nothing under the Wells Fargo, but behind a pier under the post office, he spotted a bag of some sort.

Dropping to his hands and knees, he crawled through the mud and reached for the bag. His hand froze. Beneath the black handle was a name stenciled in white, Doctor Samuel Walton Sears.

Back at the jail, Josh dropped the bag on the table in front of the sheriff. "Get your coat on, Mike. I'll get our ponies." He turned to the sheriff. "I found Doc Sears' satchel under the post office. Somebody's been lying to us, Sheriff. I got me a feeling, it's that corporal. I'm going to get Mike to show me where he saw those jaspers. Maybe I'll find something out there."

Sheriff Rabb grimaced. "Do you think . . ." He shook his head.

Josh blew through his lips. "Lord, I hope not."

Josh found more than he wanted.

Doc Sears' corpse lay half-covered under a snow bank, and wild animals and birds had begun to dispose of those limbs exposed by the melting snow.

After lashing the doctor across his saddle, Josh led the buckskin while Mike Gray-Eyes pointed out the mesquite from behind which he had watched the small party of men around the fire.

Casting about from the back of his pony, Mike Gray-Eyes cut sign of about five or six ponies heading southeast. Josh knelt and studied the tracks, which were three-quarters filled with water. Beneath the canopy of liveoak leaves, the tracks remained clear in the unmelted snow.

"About a day." Josh frowned up at Mike Gray-Eyes. "But they're going away from town, not toward it."

The old Indian warrior grunted, a wry twist to his thin lips. Josh nodded. "This trail was made later, when they were leaving. That's what you're saying?"

Mike Gray-Eyes nodded.

"The gold," the young deputy muttered, glancing at the sheriff as the two headed back along the boardwalk to the jail after leaving Doc Sears at the Tonsorial

Parlor where the barber doubled as the undertaker. "It had to be the gold, Sheriff. Doc must have stumbled on to them while they were either going in or coming out. And it had to be one of these Confederate boys, probably the Corporal. He was on sentry duty at two o'clock at the rear of Wells Fargo. He said so himself."

When they reached McCool's Saloon, they cut across the street. "Blast this crutch," the sheriff muttered, hobbling through the ankle deep mud. "Anyway, it he did catch them moving the gold, why didn't they just make up some kind of fancy story for him. They could have told him they were transferring the gold or something." He nodded back in the direction of the undertaker's. "Doc would've believed that. He would have had no reason not to."

Josh shook his head as he pushed open the thick slab door to the jail. "But what if he recognized someone, someone here in town who couldn't afford to be identified? Someone who didn't belong at Wells Fargo? A Copperhead. And who better than Lester Boles?" He looked around at Mike Gray-Eyes sitting in front of the pot-bellied stove and added. "The man-who-white-people-give-writing."

With a frown knitting his forehead, Sheriff Rabb glanced at Mike Gray-Eyes. "Even if you're right, you still got a problem, Josh. Nobody is going to believe an Indian over a white man. All Boles has to do is deny he was anywhere near those others." He glanced at Mike Gray-Eyes. "No disrespect intended, but that's just how things are."

Josh studied the sheriff several moments. "Then I reckon we'll have to make Boles show his hand.

Sheriff Rabb arched an eyebrow. "Oh? How do you figure on doing that?"

The deputy nodded out the window. "Word's already spread about Doc. Here comes Lester Boles and Amos Dunlop." He motioned to Mike Gray-Eyes. "Get out the back. Keep an eye on Boles when he leaves here, understand?"

The old Kickapoo grunted.

"So what do you have in mind?" the sheriff asked after Mike closed the door behind him.

A crooked grin played over Josh's lips. "I'll explain later, but right now, I plan to lie a lot. Just play along."

At that moment, the door burst open. Stunned disbelief etched lines in both men's faces. "Is it true, Sheriff," asked Lester Boles. "Doc Sears is dead!"

"Afraid so, boys. Josh found him out east of town."

"But . . . but, how? Why? Who did it?" Amos Dunlop, the Wells Fargo agent stammered.

Josh studied the two men. The astonished expressions on their faces appeared sincere, too sincere to be contrived. He glanced at the sheriff and a knowing look passed between them. "It was the gold, boys," Josh said. "Doc stumbled on some jaspers carrying the gold from your office, Amos. They killed him before he could spread the alarm."

Amos' face darkened. "Impossible!" He nodded to the sheriff. "You saw the strongbox in the safe yourself, Sheriff. No one took it. Why, the cavalry captain hisself identified the strongbox. I was there this morning when they moved it out."

Suddenly, the shaky story Josh had put together grew considerably more solid when he heard Amos's remarks. "Because, Amos," the deputy replied, making a wild guess. "Whoever took the gold and killed Doc switched boxes, which meant they had a key to not only your office, but your safe."

Lester Boles's face paled. He swallowed hard, an almost imperceptible reaction, but one Josh spotted. "How . . . how do you know all that, Deputy. Did you see them?"

"I didn't, but we have a witness who did."

The postmaster's jaw dropped open. He glanced around the empty jail. "A witness? Who?"

Josh shook his head, and the sheriff spoke up. "He's hid away, Lester. For safekeeping. We've already sent word to the cavalry. I expect them back here within a few hours and then we'll get on the trail of the gold."

Amos Dunlop shook his head. "I can't believe it, Sheriff. I'm the only one with keys. Who could have done it? How did they get keys?"

Josh shook his head. "That's what we can't figure out. Other than the cavalry, did either of you see any strangers in town?"

Lester Boles swallowed hard once again. "No, but I was at the box dinner all day. You remember that, Deputy. I was the one who auctioned off all the boxes. I was there all day. You can ask the preacher."

"Yeah. I remember. What about you, Amos?"

The Wells Fargo agent shook his head. "Nothing out of the ordinary. At least, not as far as I can remember. I left the box dinner about four." He looked at the diminutive postmaster. "Lester was still there."

The postmaster spoke up. "You know that sometimes some mighty rough hardcases hangs out over to McCool's. Might have been some of those jaspers." He paused, then added, "Did your witness describe any of them?"

"Yep, but they don't ring a bell with me," Sheriff Rabb replied. "He said one hombre rode into the camp late."

The postmaster caught his breath. "Did . . . did he see him? I mean, could he describe him?"

Sheriff Rabb shook his head. "No. He was so close to the camp, he was afraid to look. Afraid those owl-hoots would spot him."

Suppressing a grin, Josh nodded. "That's what I figure too."

"I'll ride out in a posses with you, Sheriff," Amos volunteered. He paused and grinned sheepishly at the sheriff's broken leg. "I mean, with the deputy."

"Yeah, me too. I'll ride with you," Boles said. "Just say when."

"Thanks, boys," Josh replied. "I'll send word."

Chapter Twenty-one

J osh turned to the sheriff after Boles and Dunlop left. "What do you think?"

"Hard to say. They both looked surprised. I've knowed them boys for years, and I don't figure either of them is that good a play-actor. In their favor though, they was both at the box dinner. You heard Amos. Lester was still there when he left around four o'clock." He gave Josh a crooked grin. "It ain't possible for a jasper to be two places at once, the church and behind Wells Fargo."

"Maybe so, but did you notice Boles' face when he heard about our witness? Turned whiter than a sheet."

Rabb arched an eyebrow. "That's what puzzles me. Of course, now that I figure on it, he could have been the one Mike spotted yesterday morning, and he decided to stay in town in front of everyone while the robbery took place. What better alibi? Now what?"

Josh peered out the window. "It's going to be interesting. If he's one of the Copperheads, then you can bet he's got to get word to the others that the cavalry is coming back. At the same time, he can't close down the post office without arousing suspicion."

The sheriff's face lit with the sudden realization of what Josh was suggesting. "You figure there's more than one of them traitors around?"

A chilling thought hit Josh, one he decided best to keep to himself for the time being. "Got to be." The deputy nodded to the sheriff's busted leg. "You can't ride, so write a letter to Captain Edwards. Tell him what we suspect. I'll have Mike Gray-Eyes deliver it."

"What about you?"

"I'm going to follow Boles or whoever he sends after the gold. If he is our man," he added.

Sheriff Rabb grunted and cleared his throat. "Sounds good, but—well, reckon there's a little problem."

Still peering from the window, Josh replied over his shoulder. "What?"

"I—ah, well, truth is, I can't read or write."

Josh looked around in surprise.

The sheriff growled. "Well, it ain't no sin. I never had no need to cipher or nothing."

A grin played over Josh's lips, and he remembered how the Sheriff had paid no attention to the document Josh had written for the inquest into the death of the two Circle B punchers. "Don't worry about it, Sheriff. I'll write it out and you can make your mark. That sound okay?"

Sheriff Rabb grinned and reached for the coffee pot. "Want some?"

Standing at the window so he could keep an eye on the post office, Josh quickly scribbled out the message informing the captain of the suspicions concerning the gold and Corporal Poole. He added,

If you find that the gold is missing, follow Mike Gray-Eyes. He will cut my deputy's trail as he will be following those I believe to have the gold.

He read the message to the sheriff who laboriously made a large X at the bottom, after which Josh wrote out the sheriff's name.

Josh folded the message into an envelope. Just before he sealed it, he froze, peering out the window. "Well, well. Would you take a look at that?"

"What? What?" Sheriff Rabb shoved himself out of his chair and hobbled across the room to peer out the window with Josh. "Boles," he muttered. "And he's heading straight over to the Methodist Church."

The sheriff looked up at Josh in stunned disbelief. "Wh . . . What—" When he saw Josh shaking his head, he stammered. "You—you knew—the preacher?"

"No. Not for sure. And let's us don't jump to any conclusions, Sheriff. He might be having some other business with Reverend Adams."

Sheriff Rabb gulped. "Reckon you might be right." He blew out through his lips. "I certainly hope you're right."

Josh's eyes grew cold and hard. "I do too, Sheriff, but I got a sick feeling in the pit of my stomach that the two of them are neck deep in all this." He handed the envelope to the sheriff. "Give this to Mike. Tell him to find Captain Edwards and bring the patrol back. Tell him I'll leave a trail even a blind Kickapoo can follow.'

The old sheriff looked up at Josh in surprise. "You leaving now?"

The younger man nodded. "Just a precaution, Sheriff. I'm going to be waiting out there in the woods just in case someone gets a sudden notion to take themselves a little ride." He unfolded the bill of sale. "If something happens to me, check with Fort McKavett if the figures on this bill of sale are accurate."

"I don't understand."

"What I suspect happened was that Sonora Fats changed the number of beeves on the bill of sale, adding the rustled cows. The army paid him for the total, then he paid McCool for the ones he had originally shipped." He shrugged. "McCool gets his money, and Fats gets what's left over. I'm betting anything, Sheriff, that this bill of sale won't match the one the army has."

Rabb's face lit in understanding. "The army's will have more beeves on it."

Josh nodded. "Exactly."

"And that means McCool's got no idea what's going on here?"

"That's about the cut of it." He nodded to the window. "Now, keep an eye out there in case someone rides out while I'm gathering up my plunder."

Josh hurriedly rolled up what few pieces of chicken and cake that remained from the box dinner into an oil-cloth and jammed it in his saddlebags along with a box of .36 paper cartridges for his Colt and .44 rimfires for his Henry. He grabbed a couple blankets, canteen, and with a brief nod, disappeared out the back door.

Sheriff Rabb remained at the window. Down the street, Lester Boles emerged from the church, looked around nervously once or twice, then scurried back to the post office. The sheriff cursed. "If you're a blasted Copperhead, I'll shoot you myself, Lester!"

Moments later, the back door opened. A gust of cold air swirled inside, and then the door closed. Mike Gray-Eyes searched the room for Josh.

"He's gone, Mike. He gave me this for you." Quickly, the sheriff explained the plan. "If you ride hard, you can catch the patrol before dark, but watch out for the corporal. We figure he's one of them no-good Copperhead traitors."

Sonora Fats and his band of hardcases rode out of Fort Terrett earlier that morning, cutting south of Junction Flats, planning to intercept the gold before it reached Huntsville.

While there were two or three well-traveled roads from Kimble County eastward, Fats knew those who had taken the gold would stay off the roads, which limited their routes for they would be traveling through some of the most rugged areas of the Texas Hill Country, country cut by icy streams at the base of precipitous bluffs. Rocky canyons stretching for miles in either direction, and if the geography was not formidable enough, the party would have to contend with renegade bands of Comanche and Apache.

Grat Plummer pulled up beside Sonora Fats. "I thought you said old man Bartholomew was pushing his herd to Kerrville."

Fats' big belly bounced up and down. "That's right. I did."

"So, what's going on? Kerrville's back south of us. We're heading to Cherry Springs this way."

Fats leered at Grat, his thick lips turning inside out like greasy sausages. "I know where it is."

Grat glanced over his shoulder at Rowdy Joe Lowe and the two drifters who were listening intently to the conversation. "We want to know what you got in mind, Fats." Plummer's voice was cool.

The big man laughed. "Boys, this job is the last one. I didn't tell you before because I didn't want anyone getting drunk and opening his mouth. This one will bring us sixty-thousand dollars in gold, enough so you can go wherever you want and live like a king. Just hold your horses. You'll see what I'm talking about."

"Sixty-thousand?" Grat Plummer whistled. His eyes narrowed. "How are we splitting it?"

Fats laughed. "I figured on equal shares if you boys got no objection to that."

Behind him, Rowdy Joe Lowe guffawed. "Not one bit, Fats. Not one bit at all."

Sonora Fats grinned. Except that some shares will be more equal than others, Rowdy, he said to himself.

At the same time Sonora Fats passed several miles south of Junction Flats, Josh was backing his buckskin into a thick motte of liveoak as Reverend Matthew Adams led his horse out of the small stable behind the parsonage and swung into the saddle.

Josh frowned as the preacher headed north, keeping his horse at a gentle canter. The sign he and Mike Gray-Eyes had cut, the sign he figured was that of the Copperheads with the gold led east, not north. So, if the preacher were one of the Copperheads, why was he heading north instead of east?

He glanced at the post office, uncertain if he should remain where he was to see what Lester Boles would do or follow the preacher.

At that moment, a buckboard rolled in from the north road. Josh grimaced. Two riders trotted along beside the buckboard and bouncing on the seat, bundled against the cold, was Mary Simmons.

That made up Josh's mind. He reined Buck around and pointed him north. The last thing he needed now was any kind of interference, regardless of the good intentions behind it.

He rode slowly through the live oak. The preacher was out of sight, but Josh knew that he could cut the reverend's sign whenever he had a mind. He wanted to give Matt Adams some more space so the preacher wouldn't accidentally spot Josh tagging along behind.

And yet, if the parson were a Copperhead, and if he were alarmed at the fact the theft had been discovered, he might have more on his mind than the possibility of being followed.

After fifteen minutes, Josh cut to his left, intersecting the trail left by the preacher. Ten minutes later, Josh stiffened, his eyes instantly spotting the lengthening stride of Adams' horse as the preacher pushed the animal into an all-out gallop.

Holding Buck into a slow walk, Josh studied the tracks for over a quarter-of-a-mile, noting with satisfaction that the Reverend Adams had glued himself firmly to the saddle, not once looking over his shoulder.

Had he scooted around in the saddle, the pony's tracks would have indicated a shift in weight. Best Josh could tell without the keen eyes of Mike Gray-Eyes, the preacher kept his weight in one spot, in the middle of the saddle and leaning over his pony's neck.

Abruptly, the trail turned east. A triumphant grin spread over Josh's face as he leaned forward and patted his buckskin's neck. "Looks like we figured right, Buck. That blasted preacher is a Copperhead traitor."

"He's been here before," Josh muttered sometime later, noting how Adams' trail wound through canyons, along streams, around rugged hills, by-passing all obstacles that might have forced him to backtrack and cut a new trail.

As Josh rode, he did some figuring. It had been almost twenty-four hours since the theft of the gold. The previous day had been overcast, so the Copperheads probably rode until after dark and pushed out at first light. Counting four hours yesterday and eight so far today, they'd been traveling twelve hours, maybe fifty or sixty miles, right close to Cherry Springs.

He glanced up. The clouds had broken and patches of blue shone through. If there were a moon tonight, the Copperheads might ride on through the night.

"Well, Buck," he said above the pounding the buckskin's hooves. "I don't know about those jaspers, but I'll bet whatever you want that the preacher don't let the night stop him."

From time to time, the preacher eased up on his pony, giving the animal a chance to breathe. Josh couldn't help appreciating the preacher, even if he were a Copperhead, for not driving his horse too hard. On the other hand, he told himself, it was a purely practical decision for if the horse broke down, Adams couldn't get word to the Copperheads about the discovery of the theft.

The clouds continued to blow away. Back to the west, the sun eased down on the horizon when suddenly, half-a-dozen shots echoed from the rugged hills to the east.

Josh reined up and listened. The hills echoed with the

sharp cracks of a revolver followed by the heavier booming of rifles. "What in the Sam Hill is going on?" Josh muttered, easing his buckskin forward at a slow walk.

Buck's ears were perked forward, and the animal's dark eyes quartered the forest before him.

"Hold on, boy," Josh whispered, reining up. The gunfire was coming from just beyond the next rocky hill. He dismounted and tied Buck to a live oak and shucked his Henry.

Quietly, he crept to the crest of the hill where he fell to his belly and peered into the shallow basin below. Despite the shadows spilling across the valley, he recognized the preacher's horse, lying on its side, blood spurting from the animal's neck.

Chapter Twenty-two

A few yards beyond the dying pony, Reverend Matthew Adams crouched behind a craggy boulder. As the deputy watched, the preacher fired at a shadow on the side of the hill just below Josh.

Two rifles boomed from below. Josh squinted into the shadows and spotted four Indians hunkered behind boulders and thick trunks of ancient liveoaks.

Suddenly, horses whinnied. Josh cursed. The Indian ponies must have scented Josh's buckskin. One of the Indians looked back up the hill. Comanche! When he spotted Josh, he shouted a war cry, but the challenge died in his throat as a two hundred grain slug pushed by twenty-six grains of black powder blew the back of his head off.

Swinging the muzzle to the right, Josh pumped slug after slug into the shadows where the other Comanches had hidden. Startled shouts broke the encroaching darkness, followed by bodies crashing through under-brush, and finally the distant beat of hooves clattering over the rocky ground. Josh counted two. What about the third Comanche? Where was he?

Josh rolled to his right several feet, coming to rest behind a scrubby oak on the crest of the hill. The night had fallen silent, and darkness pooled in the valley below.

From the pitch-black basin at the base of the hill, a voice called out. "Hello up there!"

"Quiet!" Josh hissed. He cocked the Henry, settled the butt into his shoulder, and waited. Having no wood-en forearm, the barrel and loading tube of the Yellow Boy Henry was blistering to the touch.

After a few minutes, crickets chirruped, and the sounds of the night returned. In the distance, a coyote howled. Still Josh lay without moving, and then he heard the soft scratching of leather against rock off to his left. He pulled back into the sparse shadows cast by the oak and waited, squinting into the night.

As his eyes grew accustomed to the darkness, he began to discern the nebulous shapes of shrubs and small scrub oak against a background of glittering stars. He flexed his cramped fingers about the trigger and loading tube of the rifle, expecting at any moment for Reverend Adams to call out once again.

The slight sounds came once again, like the rustle of a spider over dry leaves, then stopped. In his mind's eyes, Josh pictured the crouching Comanche, easing forward one, two steps, then freezing while his keen eyes tried to penetrate the night, then moving once again, each time at a different oblique angle.

Holding his breath, Josh strained to pick up any sound, and then he heard the faint scratching again, this time punctuated by the rattle of a limestone cobble that shifted under the weight of the Comanche's foot.

The sound ceased immediately, then started once again. One second, Josh was gazing past a dark shrub, and in the next, a second object appeared just beyond the first, blotting out a few stars.

Josh eased the muzzle of the Henry to the left. The darkness was too complete to sight, so he pointed the barrel at the dark object and squeezed the trigger.

The sudden explosion ripped the silence of the night apart, and the orange fire spitting from the muzzle illumined the startled face of the Comanche.

Like a sledgehammer pounding into a hog's skull, the two hundred grain slug slammed into the Comanche. There came a sharp grunt from the darkness, and then the sound of a body falling to the ground followed by a death gurgle rattling in the Comanche's throat.

And then silence.

Josh remained in the shadows, waiting.

Soon, a waning moon rose, and from where he lay, Josh saw the dead Comanche not fifteen feet from him. He peered into the darkness below. He started to call out to the preacher, then hesitated. He didn't have any concrete proof against Reverend Adams, although the circumstantial evidence was more than enough to convince Josh on the preacher's guilt.

He decided to play his cards close to the vest for the time being. Chalk the meeting up to chance. "Hello, down there? Are you all right?"

After a moment, a voice replied, "Who's that up there?"

"Josh Barkley. I'm the deputy over in Junction Flats. I was heading for Cherry Springs when I heard the shooting."

An excited voice shouted back. "Barkley! Am I glad to hear that. It's me, Reverend Adams."

"Preacher? What the Sam Hill are you doing out here?"

The reverend hesitated. "Riding over to Laurel Woods to pay a visit to the minister there, George Evans."

Josh rose to his feet. "Well, come on up, Preacher. Grab your gear from your pony. I spotted a little hidey-hole where we can put up for the night."

"What about the Indians?"

"Dead or gone. Now come on up."

Ten minutes later, the two had settled beneath a limestone overhang. They faced each other from either side of a small fire. Reverend Adams had a lazy grin on his face, but a wary look in his eyes as if Josh's sudden appearance was a little too convenient. "Well, Deputy, you coming along was sure a blessing."

The preacher was fishing, which meant he was suspicious of Josh's sudden presence. Well, the deputy told himself, two could play the same game. He could do a little fishing of his own, just be careful of what you say, he cautioned himself. "Reckon it was, Preacher. From what I've been told, the main road own south to Laurel Woods would have saved you a heap of miles."

The reverend gave Josh a sheepish grin. "Of course, you're right, but I had a church member to visit first."

Josh nodded. Another lie. He unrolled the oilskin from the grub he had packed and offered the reverend some cold chicken. "Coffee would be mighty tasty, but the Comanche can pick up smells a mile away."

"Water's good for me. You say, you're going over to Cherry Springs, huh?" He asked, quickly changing the subject.

A frown knit Josh's brows. He decided to mix a little fact with fiction. He watched the preacher carefully. "Yep. Kinda wish I wasn't though. Reckon you heard about Doc Sears, huh?"

Reverend Adams looked at Josh, the puzzled expression on his face exuding pure innocence. "Doc? No. What about him?"

It was Josh's turn to play the innocent. "Really? You must've left town early. He's dead."

"He's what?"

If Josh hadn't known better, he would have been taken in by the preacher's contrived shock. He nodded, his green eyes trying to interpret every expression on the preacher's face. "That's right. Wells Fargo was robbed. Whoever did it killed Doc. He must've stumbled on them while they were carrying out the gold."

He nodded to the east. "Doc had family in Cherry Springs. I was going over to notify them."

A sly look slid across Adams' face, then vanished as quickly as it had appeared. "I didn't know Doc had family in Cherry Springs. He never mentioned it to me."

Josh shrugged in an effort to appear nonchalant. "Can't prove it by me. The sheriff told me to notify an old boy named Edgar Potter. He's a cousin." He yawned and stretched. "Well, reckon we best get some shuteye. First thing in the morning, we'll see if we can catch you one of those Indian ponies."

He lay down and pulled his blankets over his shoulder. He hoped he hadn't made a mistake by trying to finesse the preacher. If he were wrong, if the preacher saw through Josh's subterfuge, he could wake up staring at six feet of dirt.

He lay facing the preacher, feigning sleep with his hand beneath the blankets resting on the butt of his Colt.

Long after the fire had died out, Matthew Adams lay staring into the darkness over his head, not quite certain that he believed the deputy's story. Yet, Josh had given no indication that he suspected the preacher of any collaboration with any crime. Maybe he was doing just exactly what he said, riding to Cherry Springs to notify one of Doc's cousins. Besides, only a jasper with a clear conscience could be sleeping as soundly as the deputy.

His own story would hold up for there was indeed a minister in Laurel Woods, and his name was George

Evans, and he would support anything Adams said for he was the Copperhead contact in that small village. No, Adams had cleverly covered his tracks. If he had admitted he had known of Doctor Sear's death, then he could have been called upon to explain why he had left town; why he had not remained to conduct his friend's funeral.

Reverend Adams rolled over and pulled the blanket up around his neck. Sometimes when a jasper had two choices, neither of them was worth a pail of warm spit.

Should he continue his charade with the deputy until Cherry Springs where they would part or should he give him a lead plum he couldn't digest? Matt Adams drifted off to sleep while trying to decide.

Next morning, Josh searched the hillsides for the Indian ponies, at the same time trying to figure out just what his next move should be. The preacher didn't appear suspicious, but Josh knew better than to push his luck. The smart move would be to part with the preacher in Cherry Springs, and then follow him.

He found the ponies in a grassy meadow that ended abruptly at a precipitous drop off to a deep pool of icy water thirty feet below. Quickly he roped one and tied it to a shrub near the rim of the bluff so he could catch the second one. He glanced back up at the camp. The preacher was watching. Josh waved, and the preacher waved back.

When Josh turned back to the second pony, Matthew Adams, his mind made up, narrowed his eyes and slipped his Henry from the boot beneath the saddle fender. He rested it on a limb of a small live oak to steady his aim. The shot was downhill, so he aimed low. He grimaced. "Sorry, Deputy. It's you or me." Gently, he squeezed off a shot.

The saddle horn exploded in front of Josh, ripping the reins from his hands. He jerked back in surprise just as his buckskin, squealing in fright, reared and pawed at the clouds overhead. Josh tumbled off the rump of his pony and slammed to the ground on the rim of the drop off.

With a grunt, he scrabbled around, clawing at the ground.

In the next instant, he felt himself falling through the air.

Clenching his teeth, he muttered a curse, steeling himself for the impact.

He slammed into the water on his back. The force stung his flesh, and the icy water engulfed him as he plummeted several feet into the depths of the pool.

Flailing at the water, he struggled back to the surface, choking and coughing. Nothing seemed broken. He looked up, then quickly swam for the base of the bluff overlooking the pool, hoping to find a niche in which he could press himself when the preacher looked down.

The vertical wall was smooth, but a few feet to his right, he discovered a slight overhang only inches above the water. By bending his head back, he could ease under the overhang and still have room to breathe.

From the corner of his eye, he spotted his hat being swept ice-cold from the ice-cold pool by the current onto the far shore of the pool.

The icy water chilled him. Shivers racked his body uncontrollably. But he remained beneath the overhang.

Suddenly the surface of the pool exploded as the crack of a rifle broke the murmuring of the small stream. Two more shots, then silence.

Josh remained beneath the overhang.

Finally, his entire body shivering, his muscles cramped, he eased from under the overhang and peered up. All he saw was blue sky and clouds.

He pushed out into the pool and swam with the current to the shallows near the rapids downstream of the pool.

Clambering out of the icy stream, he grabbed his water-soaked Stetson and stumbled into the thick underbrush lining the stream and dropped to his belly. "Now," he muttered, studying the steep limestone walls stretching above him. "All I got to do is find a way out of here."

Chapter Twenty-three

By the time Josh scaled the thirty-foot limestone bluff, sweat was pouring from muscles that had been trembling with icy chills only minutes earlier.

He paused before climbing over the rim, peering across the valley for any sign of the preacher. Seeing nothing, he hastily pulled himself over the rim and dashed for the cover of the understory vegetation at the edge of the forest.

He lay on his belly for several minutes under a tangle of blackberry and baneberry vines studying the meadow. A distant whinny caught his attention. Across the meadow from just inside the tree line, Buck stood peering at him. Josh grinned. At least the preacher hadn't managed to catch that ornery buckskin. He whistled to the pony.

Buck didn't move.

Josh whistled again, but still the buckskin stood staring at him.

Muttering softly, Josh cut across the meadow, forcing himself to keep a soothing, gentle voice. "Easy, boy. Just keep standing there. Don't move, fella. That's it. Good boy. Don't move, or I swear, I'll shoot you between the eyes, you no-good, cantankerous broomtail," he added in a soft, almost sweet voice.

Buck perked his ears forward and flicked his black tail, but to Josh's surprise, the buckskin remained motionless.

Taking the reins, Josh paused to inspect the shattered saddle horn. From the corner of his eye, he saw Buck cut his head sharply toward him, his lips drawn back over bared teeth.

Josh jumped back and popped the horse across the muzzle with the reins, and promptly proceeded to blister the horse's skin with a string of vituperative and abusing profanity.

Finally, he swung into the saddle and glared down at the buckskin. "Just wait until I get you back to Junction Flats, you mangy piece of horseflesh. I'm going to sell you to the first drummer that comes through town."

The preacher's trail was clear as spring water, cutting directly southeast from their camp. Josh followed at a gallop, keeping his eyes forward, anticipating a possible ambush.

Best he could figure, the preacher was bypassing

Cherry Springs. "That ain't no surprise," he muttered to Buck. "Is it?"

The trail led around rugged bluffs of limestone, across icy streams, and through woodlands of live oak. From time to time, movement caused Josh to rein up only to see spooked deer racing through the forest, a forest that strangely reminded him of the one back in Georgia where he fought his last battle for the South. He drew a deep breath, and the guilt that had nagged at him for almost a year fell away when he said, "I reckon I'll go back when this is over, Buck. I hope you're up to a hard ride."

The buckskin snorted and bobbed his head up and down.

At noon, Josh cut the trail of several riders. "The gold," he muttered, studying the ground, noting how the unshod tracks of the preacher's Indian pony had fallen in with the others. "Has to be," he muttered. "Who else is this far out in the middle of nowhere?"

Dismounting, Josh inspected the sign. The unshod tracks were sharper than the others, which indicated the Reverend Matthew Adams was still behind the party with the gold. Before mounting, Josh made a cut in the trunk of a live oak, blazing the trail for Mike Gray-Eyes.

He swung back into the saddle, and with a click of his tongue, Josh pushed Buck into a canter, studying the sign and constantly quartering the hills and forests ahead.

An hour later, Josh reined up and sniffed the air. Wood smoke. Instantly, he pulled off the trail, halting behind a low-sprawling oak. The rocky hills and thick stands of live oaks twisted the breeze until it was next to impossible to discern the direction from which the wood smoke came.

He guessed the source of the smoke was back to the northeast, beyond a string of rugged hogback ridges. He dismounted, and eased forward on foot. The closer he drew to the ridges, the stronger the odor of a campfire.

He froze behind a tree trunk when he caught the aroma of boiling coffee. A grim smile played over his lips as he made his way to the top of the ridge. He removed his hat and peered over the crest.

Down below, six hombres hunkered about a fire beneath a live oak not far from the rim of a canyon, drinking coffee and gnawing on what looked like some of Mister Lincoln's shingles. Standing in front of the fire was the Reverend Matthew Adams, and beyond, tied to a low branch on an oak was a big-footed draft horse with a metal box lashed to the frame of a packsaddle.

Josh quickly sized up the camp, which was backed up to a canyon. How deep, Josh couldn't tell. A steep hogback rose beyond the camp. Josh spotted movement on the crest of the distant hill, but as he watched, a swirl of sparrows took to the air.

He turned his attention back to the camp. Six of them, seven counting the preacher, too many for him to take on himself, which meant that he would have to follow and wait for the right opportunity to present itself. Maybe the smart move was to simply wait until the gold was turned over to the next contact, and the band of Copperheads returned to their homes.

He slid down the ridge and hurried back to his pony. "Mike, where in the blazes are you?" he muttered, peering into the woodlands to the west.

On the distant hogback, Grat Plummer whispered. "You see that hombre on the hill yonder, Fats?"

Sonora Fats grunted. "Yep."

"You reckon he's one of them?"

The fat outlaw snorted. "Ain't likely. Else why would he be up there and not down with them others?"

"Maybe he's a lookout."

"Maybe."

Grat shrugged. "So, now what? We jump them?"

Fats studied the small band below. His eyes narrowed as they swept over his younger brother. A blasted hypocrite! No better than a blasted liar! Playing the preacher when he ain't no better than a traitor. "Not yet. We'll wait and see about that other jasper. Could be just a drifter that don't want no truck with nobody."

"He might be a scout for another bunch."

"Could be. We'll just wait and see."

As Josh swung into the saddle, the birds behind him suddenly grew silent. He cocked his head, turning an ear to his back trail. Hoof beats. He stiffened, then grinned. Mike Gray-Eyes! About time, he told himself, but then he hesitated.

What if it were more Copperheads? Maybe this was where the gold was to change hands.

With a grimace, Josh quickly moved off the trail. He would wait until whomever was coming passed, and then fall in behind. It would be easier to follow a dozen hombres than half that number.

He peered through the tangle of limbs.

He counted three riders, their features hidden by the leaves of the low hanging branches. He tightened the reins, backing Buck farther off the trail. Abruptly, he froze, then, recognizing the Simmons, dug his heels into the buckskins' flanks, driving him toward the trail.

The deputy yanked off his John B. and waved it wildly as he hit the trail and raced toward the oncoming riders still fifty yards distant.

The three riders reined up. Josh recognized Arch Simmons right off. Behind him rode Kelt, and then . . . He gaped, unable to believe his eyes. Beside Kelt rode Mary Simmons. Josh slid his buckskin to a halt.

Before any of them could say a word, he waved them off the trail. "Over here. Quick."

Mary started to protest, but Josh silenced her. "And be quiet. All of you."

Back in a stand of stunted scrub oak, Josh reined around to face them. He demanded. "What are you'all doing here? Where's Mike and those cavalry boys?"

Mary rode closer, the features of her heart-shaped face taut with worry. "Are you all right, Josh?" She took in his battered clothes and the two-day beard on his face.

Arch Simmons growled. "We heard about Doc Sears. The sheriff said you was on the trail of one of them Copperheads. We come to help as soon as we heard."

A mixture of gratitude and apprehension washed over Josh. He glanced over their back trail. "What about the cavalry? Mike Gray-Eyes went after them."

Kelt rode forward. "Ain't seen them, Josh. We rode into town and the sheriff told us what happened. Is it true that the preacher and Lester Boles is Copperheads, traitors?"

Mary's face paled. "I can't believe it about the preacher. He's always been a decent man."

Josh studied them a moment. Had he a choice, he'd have opted for the cavalry, but he didn't. He'd have to go with what he had. He nodded behind him. "There's a ridge a good piece back east. The preacher and Lee Rohmann are camped with five other jaspers and the Confederate gold." He paused and smiled sadly at Mary. "I don't know how else to say it, Miss Mary, but the preacher is one of them. He's a Copperhead."

"Is he the no-account what killed Doc?" Arch Simmon's craggy face was cold with anger.

"No. I don't think he knew Doc was dead until Lester Boles told him. In fairness to the preacher, that wasn't in the plans. Only the gold."

Kelt Simmons shucked his six-gun, spun the cylinder,

and slammed it back in the holster. "You say him and the gold is over that ridge yonder? How many of them?"

"Seven."

An easy smile played over the angular features of the young cowpoke's face. "Is that all? Why, lordy, Josh, we got them jaspers outnumbered."

Josh cut his eyes to Mary. "Not you. You stay back. The three of us can handle that bunch, especially if we get the jump on them."

Her eyes narrowed. She stuck out her jaw. "I'll have you know, Deputy, I can outshoot any of my brothers. You'll have to tie me up to keep me out of this fight."

Josh's temper flared. He glared at her. Last thing he needed now was a stubborn woman, but her sassiness raised the bristles on the back of his neck. "Well, little Missy, I just might do that."

She glared back at him, her eyes blazing, her jaw set. "You aren't big enough."

Her Pa and brother eased their ponies backward a step.

Josh started to dismount, but Mary said, "I'll scream if you lay one hand on me."

Arch cleared his throat. "She means it, son. Best you let her have her way. I ain't never seen a woman as hard-headed, or as good with a Henry rifle," he added.

She smiled sweetly at her father. "Thank you kindly, Pa."

Kelt gave Josh a knowing grin.

The deputy knew when he was whipped. He shook his head, glaring into the fire shooting from her eyes.

"All right. I don't like it, but I know when I'm licked. So, now listen. That ridge yonder overlooks the camp. We can spread out along it. Hide behind the boulders and trees. If we're lucky, we can get the jump on them."

"What if we're not? What if they spot us?" Kelt eyed Josh.

"We got good cover on the ridge. They got a canyon behind them, and a steep hogback on the other side. It isn't a spot I would have picked to camp, especially if I was running with sixty thousand dollars of Confederate gold."

"What about our horses?" Arch asked.

"We'll dismount and tie them at the bottom of the ridge. That way we'll have them close if things don't go our way." He paused and shucked his Henry. "Make sure you're fully loaded. If they draw down on us when I call out, then cut loose." He glanced at Mary whose face had paled. She swallowed hard.

Arch spoke up. "I don't reckon they'll come peaceable, Deputy. Ever' last one of them is traitors, and there ain't no doubt in my mind they know what happens to traitors in this part of the country."

Josh spoke gently to Mary. "You don't have to go with us."

She swallowed hard, cut her eyes to her pa and brother, then back to Josh. "I know, but I'm going. Besides, maybe they'll give up."

Chapter Twenty-four

T he Copperheads didn't give up.

Josh called out for the seven to throw up their hands, but even before the echo of his command died out, the basin erupted with gunfire.

The blazing barrage from the crest of the ridge was murderous. Two hundred grain lead slugs ripped apart the camp. The campfire exploded as slugs tore into it. The coffeepot shot ten feet in the air.

The Copperheads scrabbled to duck behind the live oaks and return fire. The deadly fire cut down two before they reached the protection of the thick trunks of the ancient trees.

The sudden outbreak of gunfire startled the horses. Squealing in fear, they reared back, jerking on the ropes. The draft sorrel with the gold fought against the thick rope snubbing her to an ancient and gnarled oak.

After the first burst of gunfire, Josh called out, "Adams. This is Barkley. We got you pinned down. Throw out your guns and come out with your hands over your heads."

His answer was a sharp crack of a rifle and a slug exploded in the limestone inches from his head, peppering his face with fragments of yellow limestone.

Josh jerked back, his cheek stinging. Mary jerked around, staring at him, her eyes wide. "Josh! Are you hurt?"

He shook his head.

The young woman's eyes blazed. She clenched her teeth and muttered a couple unladylike, but appropriate expressions as she leaped to her feet and raked the camp below with bullets. "That'll teach you a thing or two," she shouted, ducking back behind a boulder just before half-a-dozen slugs splatted against the boulder. She quickly reloaded the Henry.

Slugs cut the air like angry bees. Josh shouted. "Keep that blond head down, you hear?"

Mary grinned at him.

Smoke from the shattered campfire and ball and cap six-guns rolled up the ridge, stinging Josh's eyes.

Suddenly, Kelt cried out and spun to the ground, clutching his shoulder.

Arch roared. "Kelt!"

The young man rolled over and grimaced. "I'm all right."

Infuriated, the old rancher jumped to his feet and emptied his saddle gun into the thick smoke below. A voice cried out in pain.

One of the Copperheads burst out of the smoke and made a dash for the ponies. He swung into the saddle, but before he could dig his spurs into the pony's flanks, a slug from Arch Simmons' rifle knocked the traitor from the saddle. "That'll teach you," Arch shouted. "You bunch of no-account traitors."

The Copperhead squirmed on the ground, trying to reach the protection of a nearby boulder. One of his partners raced to his side, only to catch a lead plum in his leg, sending him sprawling to the ground.

Then another shouted. "Hold up. We give up. Don't shoot." It was Matt Adams.

Josh whispered harshly to Mary and Arch. "Stay where you are, and keep your guns on them." He shouted to the camp. "Throw your guns out, then show yourself, hands over your heads.

Only one sidearm hit the ground. "I said all of them," Josh shouted.

"That's all. The others are hurt bad," the preacher replied. "I'm coming out. Don't shoot."

"Come on out, Preacher."

Hands over his head, Matthew Adams stepped from behind a live oak and stopped beside the campfire.

"Where are the others?" Arch Simmons shouted.

"Behind me. Bad hurt."

Josh eased to the end of the ridge, then called out. "You others. Crawl out, or we'll start shooting."

"We're coming, we're coming."

Moments later, three cowpokes crawled from behind a house-sized boulder.

"Where are the other three?"

"Dead."

Josh glanced at Arch Simmons. "Let's ease down. Kelt, are you able to hold a gun on them from up here?"

The younger Simmons pushed to his feet and laid his Henry on a shelf of limestone. His left arm hung limp. "I got 'em, Josh. You all go ahead."

The deputy looked at Mary. "I don't reckon it would do any good to ask you to stay up here, would it?"

She glared at him defiantly. "No."

Arch Simmons grinned as Josh shook his head and replied. "I didn't think so." He drew a deep breath. "Well, let's go."

Slowly they eased down the slope to the camp.

On the far ridge, Sonora Fats leered. "All right, boys. Get them lawmen."

"What about the girl?" Grat Plummer whispered.

"Her too. We can't leave no witnesses behind."

From where he leaned against the limestone shelf, Kelt Simmons caught the movement on the far ridge. When he spotted the rifle muzzles slide through the serrated upthrusts in the ridges, he shouted, "Pa! Look out!" At the same time, he fired at the head protruding just above the ridge.

Down below, Matthew Adams dropped to the ground, covering his head.

Mary and Josh leaped behind the protection of rugged boulders along the canyon rim as the three rifles cut down on them from the top of the ridge. Arch remained upright, raking the crest of the ridge until a slug caught him in the side, spinning him to the ground.

The limestone boulders behind which Mary and Josh lay circled the rear of the camp, passing within a few feet of the canyon rim, and ending near the ridge from which they had been ambushed. He whispered to Mary, "Stay here. I'll slip around and come in from behind the bushwhackers."

"No," she muttered, her lips drawn tight, her eyes filled with a mixture of fear and anger. "I'm going with you."

Josh rolled his eyes. "Come on then. Just stay down." The sun beat down, baking Josh's back as he crawled on his hands and knees, the rough limestone rubbing his hands raw and wearing the knees of his trousers. He paused.

"What's wrong?" Mary whispered.

"Just listening."

"I don't hear anything."

"That's good," Josh continued crawling. "Let's go. Be careful up ahead. There's only a couple feet to the canyon rim drop-off."

Ahead was the hogback. Once there, they could work their way around to the rear slope and come up behind the bushwhackers. He glanced hastily over the boulders. The preacher still lay on the ground.

To his right, the canyon dropped away several hundred feet to a stream far below that looked more like a thin silver ribbon than a brook.

As he rounded a boulder, Josh jerked to a halt. Staring him in the face was the muzzle of a .44 six-gun. Behind the six-gun was the leering face of Sonora Fats!

Chapter Twenty-five

Sonora Fats' thick lips turned inside out when he grinned. "Where do you think you're going, Deputy?"

Mary gasped.

Josh glanced over his shoulder. Behind them stood Grat Plummer, his hatchet face twisted with a smug sneer.

Fats motioned for Josh and Mary to stand. He called over his shoulder. "All right, little brother. You can get up now."

Mary gasped, and Josh gaped when Matthew Adams pushed himself to his feet. "Brother?" Josh choked out.

"Reckon so, but he don't claim me, Deputy." Sarcasm oozed from Fat's words. "He's too busy going around being a preacher-man and a Copperhead traitor."

Adams glared at his older brother. He dragged the tip of his tongue over his lips. "That isn't the way it is,

Elm. You know that. I'm trying to help keep the Union together."

Sonora Fats snorted. "You hear that, Deputy? My brother here says he's trying to keep the Union together." The greasy fat man hawked up a mouthful of spittle and spat it on the ground at Adams' feet. "That's what I think of you, Matthew. You're a liar and a traitor. I heard you talking to that scrawny little post office jasper. How much were you being paid for this job, twenty-five percent of the gold?"

Mary gasped.

Fats sneered. "That's right, little lady. My brother here ain't no preacher. He's a southern deserter and a spy, and not a right smart one at that. He never could figure out who did all that rustling. What about you, Deputy? You want to know who done all that rustling?"

Josh eyed the larger man, looking for a chance to make his play. "I figure I'm looking at him right now."

Grat Plummer laughed. "He ain't as dumb as he looks, Fats."

"He sure ain't."

"So, why you telling me all this?"

Fats lifted an eyebrow. "'Cause neither of you will have a chance to tell the story." He nodded to the canyon behind them. "You'll both be down there."

Matthew Adams stepped forward. "No, Elmer. You can't do that. Not to a woman."

Josh glanced at Plummer, but the killer kept Mary between him and Josh just in case the deputy tried his hand. When Plummer saw Josh size up the situation, he grinned crookedly. "You ain't got a chance, Deputy."

"Listen to me, Elmer," Adams said. "I don't care about the deputy, but you can't kill a woman. Turn her loose. You can have my share of the sixty-thousand."

Sonora Fats laughed, a mocking snort. "Your share? Don't be so stupid, little Brother. I'm taking it all." He turned his murderous gimlet eyes on Josh and Mary. "I'm going to kill them and then take the gold. I oughta kill you too, but you're family. I don't care what you do, but if you was smart, you'd hightail it out of the country."

Matthew Adams cut his eyes toward Josh and Mary, then threw himself at Sonora Fats. "No," he screamed. "I won't let you shoot her."

Grat Plummer swung his six-gun around on Adams, but the crack of a Henry cut through the commotion. The slug struck Plummer in the back. He screamed and tumbled over a small boulder, slamming into Mary Simmons and knocking her to the ground as he rolled over the rim. Frantically, he grabbed at her, pulling the frightened woman after him as he hurtled to the rocks far below.

Sliding over the rim, Mary clawed at the rocky ground, her terrified eyes searching for Josh.

He leaped for her, grabbing her wrist as she dropped over the edge, pulling him after her. With his free hand, he made a frantic stab at a thick live oak root growing from the side of the canyon, managing to wrap his fingers around it. "Grab my belt," he gasped, feeling his fingers slowly opening. "Hurry. I'm losing my grip."

The frightened young woman grabbed Josh's belt and clung to him like black on a cast-iron skillet.

The deputy managed to grasp the root with both hands and then he heard two shots followed by a soft moan. He looked up into the sneering grin of Sonora Fats standing on the canyon rim, staring down at them.

"This is one to brag on," Fats laughed. "Two with one shot. You can join my little brother, and then I'll take care of that one up on the hill." He cocked his six-gun and swung the muzzle around toward the deputy.

Josh clenched his teeth. With a Herculean effort, he threw himself up, and with one arm, swung at Sonora Fats' ankles, knocking his legs from under him. In the next second, Josh grabbed at the root in a desperate effort to keep them from falling.

Fats screamed and bounced over the side. He grabbed futilely at Josh and Mary as he plummeted past them.

He screamed all the way down to the rocks several hundred feet below.

For long seconds, Josh clung to the root, trying to catch his breath. He felt Mary's fingers flexing about his belt. Finally, he managed to gasp. "I can't pull us up."

"W—what are we going to do, Josh?"

"You're going to have to climb over me."

"What?"

"You heard me. Climb up over me. And hurry. My fingers are slipping."

"All right. If you say so."

She reached up and grabbed a handful of his vest, and then she grabbed the collar of his shirt, cutting off his breath.

He choked and coughed as the nimble young woman slowly clambered up his lanky frame, jamming her boot heels in his side, almost twisting an ear off, and finally standing on his shoulders to climb onto the rim of the canyon. "Now, give me your hand," she said, her face flushed, her eyes wide with fear as she reached for him.

Finally, Josh rolled over the rim of the canyon and lay gasping for breath. He felt hands on his face and opened his eyes.

Mary was on her knees at his side, looking down at him with soft, warm eyes. "You saved my life."

"You saved mine."

She leaned over and touched her lips to his. She lifted her head, but he pulled her back and kissed her once again.

For several moments, the two stared at each other.

A rough voice growled. "Since you two seem to admire each other so much, then I reckon you best get yourselves hitched up."

Josh and Mary looked around into the smiling faces of Arch and Kelt Simmons who were leaning on each other and clutching their bloody wounds. "Wouldn't you say so, Kelt?"

Kelt's grin grew wider. "Yes, sir, Pa. I certainly would."

Josh frowned and sat up. "Sounds good to me, but

first, I've got some unfinished chores to take care of before I can talk about that. Might take a spell."

Mary glanced at her Pa, who grunted and muttered. "You talking about the war, Son?"

Dumbfounded, Josh nodded. "How—how . . ."

"The sheriff told us," Mary explained. "He thought—"

Her Pa interrupted. "Look Josh, August John knows how you two feel about each other even if you don't. He also told us what you had on your mind about joining back up."

Josh looked up into Mary's eyes. "I'm sorry."

Arch shook his head. "No need to be, son. For all practical purposes, the war's over. Useless to go back."

"What?" Josh looked at him in surprise.

"Yep. When we was with the sheriff, word come in that the Yankee army under General Sherman's orders burned Atlanta last month." His craggy face grew somber. "The South ain't got nothing left. By the time you get back, you'll be meeting our southern boys coming home to start all over."

Mary laid her slender hand on his arm. "You did more than your share for the South, Josh. Now's the time to do for yourself."

He glanced up at Arch and Kelt who were grinning like foxes in the henhouse. Nodding slowly, he rose to his feet and helped Mary to hers. He took her in his arms, a crooked grin on his face. "Maybe I should, but first, I want you to understand one thing right off. You might be able to outshoot and outride your brothers.

You might be a tomboy, but I wear the pants in my family." He jabbed his forefinger to his chest for emphasis. "And that's the way it is," he added.

"Yes, sir," Mary replied softly, standing on her tiptoes and touching her lips to his. "Whatever you say."

Behind the couple, Arch and Kelt guffawed.